THE TOYS OF PRINCES

Other works by Ghislain de Diesbach

HISTORY

Les secrets du Gotha (Julliard, 1962).

George III (Berger-Levrault, 1966).

Service de France (Émile-Paul, 1972).

Histoire de l'Émigration (Grasset, 1975, et réédition Perrin, 1984).
   Couronné par l'Académie française. Prix du Nouveau Cercle.

Necker ou la faillite de la vertu (Perrin, 1978 et 1987).
   Prix du Cercle de l'Union.

Madame de Staël (Perrin, 1983).
   Bourse Goncourt de la biographie. Grand Prix des Lectrices de *Elle*.

La Princesse Bibesco, 1886–1973 (Perrin, 1986).
   Prix des Cent Libraires de Normandie.

La Double Vie de la duchesse Colonna 1836–1879 (Perrin, 1988).

IN COLLABORATION WITH ROBERT GROUVEL

Échec à Bonaparte (Perrin, 1980).
   Couronné par l'Académie française.

ESSAYS

Le Tour de Jules Verne en quatre-vingts livres (Julliard, 1969).
   Prix de l'académie de Bretagne.

Le Gentilhomme de notre temps (Hachette-Littérature, 1972).

NOVELS

Iphigénie en Thuringe, nouvelles (Julliard, 1960).

Un joli train de vie (Julliard, 1962).
   Prix Cazes.

Le Grand Mourzouk (Julliard, 1969).

■■■■■■■■■■■■■■■■■■■■■■■■■■■■■■■■■■■■■

THE TOYS OF PRINCES

Ghislain de Diesbach

Translated from the French by

Richard Howard

TURTLE POINT PRESS

First published in France as *Iphigénie en Thuringe*
© 1960 by René Julliard
First English translation © 1962 by Ghislain de Diesbach
Published by Pantheon Books, a Division of Random Hourse, Inc.

© 1992 Turtle Point Press

Library of Congress Catalog Card Number: 92-81006
ISBN: 0-9627987-2-x

Design and composition by Wilsted & Taylor
Printed in the U.S.A.

Contents

Translator's Note to the Second Edition

of *The Toys of Princes*

When I translated these dozen tales, thirty years ago, their capital charm, it struck me, resided—or perhaps it was too volatile for residence, more a matter of camping out—*hovered*, then, in their period flavor, an exact administration of the tonalities of the nineteenth century, that age which so preternaturally dilated from 1789 to Sarajevo.

To recover such tonalities was, for a translator, to discover them. I would have to read certain authors, must reckon with certain locutions (there was no such thing as "horseback", there was only "riding" *ab illo tempore*). And perhaps there might be something to be gained, beyond the voices murmuring from the page, if I were to hear the originating resonance, the resounding origin? Beguiled by the accents of such giddy authority, I would brazenly look up or track down the . . . author in Paris, hoping that what I perceived as an historical pollenization in his case would afford, in mine, at least the transmission of a perfume, the contagion of a bouquet, once our encounter had been effected. That was all a translator might hope for, but it was something—something worth a visit in 1961 to the Rue Vieille du Temple, where M. de Diesbach, a worldly chap about my own age, it appeared, hovered with just the same fulgurations of style as his tales: on every (rather precarious) chair was arrayed a threadbare Hussar's tunic (the collector, on demand, would specify their regiments); on every (positively jeopardized) table lay a brace of worm-eaten Napoleonic pistols, or perhaps they had belonged to Benjamin Constant? The room flickered about me in all its authentic dilapidations, and if I was unsettled by the decor, I was soon convinced of one thing: frequentation of this author in his haunts (surely the right word) would be of no help whatever to a translator in need of a little less attestation, a little more conviction. I retreated to my Greenwich Village study (quite unembellished by military memorabilia of any kind) and produced, two years after (in every sense) M. de Diesbach's first effort, one of my own first translations of which I was proudest, gladdest, *sure*.

We never met again, though I am eager to report M. de Diesbach's many subsequent achievements, among them historical studies, critical essays, literary and artistic monographs (concerning George III, the Almanach de Gotha, Necker, Bonaparte, Jules Verne, and most grandly Mme de Staël, whose biography will come as no surprise to attentive readers of the sixth of these tales, "Iphigenia in Thuringia", which indeed furnished the title of the French edition; one of the monographs was devoted, in 1980, to the late Philippe Jullian, a friend of the author who not only wrote his own *chroniques galantes et scandaleuses* but also illustrated the Chatto & Windus edition of Proust and, more modestly, embellished our American edition with a characteristically droll jacket drawing, all scatterbrain pink and chartreuse); since *The Toys of Princes*, M. de Diesbach has produced two more works of consistently capricious fiction; and in addition various memorial enterprises (tantalizingly listed on the flyleaf of the latest works as *hors commerce*, a phrase that might be applied to the author in almost every sense).

Rereading the tales in the decades which have intervened since their translation, indeed occasionally reading them aloud to friends in order to savor the significant impropriety of the affair (the full effect of sentences like the one which constitutes the coda to "The Chevalier d'Armel's Wedding" can best be obtained *viva voce*; try it for yourself: "In the course of time the Grand Duchess Wilhelmine presented her husband with six sons, each handsomer than the next, and the royal pair lived long enough to be driven from their thrones by a revolution"), I find the abiding fascination of these fictions to be in their entanglement with *difference*, which we know to be the source of every narrative impulse. Differences of gender, differences of milieu, and differences of generation: the scandal that our desires are not the same, the outrage that our upbringings have alienated us from each other as well as from ourselves, the daily strangeness of growing up today with a father who had grown up yesterday, or even—in the case of several mothers in these tales—the day before that! Such are the pervasive vivacities which, beyond any superficial nomenclatural *Verfremdungseffekt*, sustain Ghislain de Diesbach's anecdotes of high life and loose living. How wonderfully they comport with those challenges to criticism which Dr Johnson lists for us, perfectly comprehending this brilliant young raconteur's initial attainment: "To remark the folly of the fiction, the absurdity of the conduct, the confusion of the names and manners of different times, and the impossibility of the events in any system of life . . ."

Richard Howard
New York, 1992

THE TOYS OF PRINCES

The Toys of Princes

■ ■ ■ IMITATING THE BAD EXAMPLE set by the subjects of ■ ■ ■
the King of France, those of the Prince-Elector of Bramberg
had overturned the Monarchy in order to proclaim the Repub-
lic. After a brief period of autonomy, the new state had been
raped by the troops of the convention, pillaged by those of the
Directory, and in 1805 it was no more than a mere department
of the French Empire, administered by a prefect who had once
been a tailor. Having taken refuge in Vienna, the Prince-
Elector Luitpold and his family were living in that city on a
modest pension granted by the Court of Austria. Several no-
blemen of his country, whose loyalty was encouraged by their
extreme poverty, formed something of a court about him,
which flattered his illusions. He had no doubt, in fact, that he
would one day reconquer his throne, and fomented intrigues
throughout Europe in order to prevail upon the other Sovereigns to furnish him means to do so. Two-thirds of his reve-
nues was spent paying secret agents in the various capitals, and
he had pawned the diamonds of his Princess in order to maintain a battalion that fought in the ranks of the Coalition. Every
morning he read the gazettes, hoping to learn that the cursed
Corsican had been murdered, and he frequently complained
that God had abandoned the House of Bramberg for the sake
of a usurper. The Elector possessed two daughters, married to
German Princes similarly dispossessed, and one son, Prince
Clément, who was about to announce his betrothal to the
Countess Georgina de Solms.

Several days before the celebration of this happy event,
Prince-Elector Luitpold received the most singular letter that

can be imagined. From the Château des Tuileries, the Grand
Master of Ceremonies, Count de Ségur, wrote that His Majesty the Emperor and King had deigned to think of young
Prince Clément in order to assure the happiness of his niece
Valérie Chirimanti. If the former Sovereign and his son were
to accept this proposition, the Emperor would restore its independence to the nation of Bramberg and declare it a kingdom over which the young pair would rule. The Prince-
Elector nearly choked with rage at Bonaparte's insolence in
daring to ally his blood to that of the Brambergs, but then he
reflected upon everything this affair could offer of advantage
to his dynasty and to his person. Although chagrined that the
crown was not offered to himself, he decided that this proposal
was not to be rejected without serious consideration. Apprised
forthwith, his secret agent in Paris sent him abundant intelligence concerning the person of Valérie Chirimanti. She was
related to the Bonapartes through the Ramolinos, who had
adopted her upon the death of her father, a poor fisherman
from the vicinity of Ajaccio, where his skiff had been sunk by
an English brig. Her mother had long been in service with the
Pozzo di Borgo family and was now living in Paris, where, to
revenge herself on Fate, she engaged domestics as the Empress
collected gowns or the Princess Pauline lovers. The Emperor
was amused by this eccentricity and had even remarked good-
naturedly, upon learning that she maintained in her employ no
less than one hundred footmen: "I shall soon have no men left
for my armies if you take them all from me thus, my cousin!"

"At least," reasoned the Prince-Elector, whose household
circumstances were sorely reduced, "at least my son shall be
waited on as he deserves to be. . . ." Valérie Chirimanti, continued the secret agent, was a young girl with the warm colouring of many Southern women, splendid black eyes, magnificent hair, and an admirable throat that aroused the jealousy
of the Emperor's own sisters. She showed dignity in her bearing, grace in her manners. Her sojourn in the celebrated insti-

tution of Madame Campan had allowed her to acquire, in proximity with the daughters of *émigrés*, that suggestion of Good Company in which the Imperial Court was so deficient. What the Prince-Elector's agent did not know was that Valérie Chirimanti was in love with an officer in the Hussars who occasionally caracoled under the windows of the Pension Campan. The two young people had seen one another, had exchanged letters, and Valérie was anxiously waiting for the officer to elope with her when the Emperor suddenly interrupted this idyll by ordering her to marry Prince Clément of Bramberg. The unfortunate girl wept so bitterly that her companions addressed a petition to the Emperor, entreating him to allow their friend to follow the dictates of her heart, but Napoleon proved obdurate and commanded his niece to take up residence in the Tuileries. Before leaving the Pension Campan where she had known, at the same time as her first transports, her first trials of love, Valérie opened the cage of her turtle-doves. Around the neck of each innocent creature she had attached a ribbon on which was embroidered the name of the beloved Hussar, and upon seeing her dreams take wing she burst into tears under the pitying eyes of the Chamberlain to whose care she was entrusted. Moved despite himself, the Emperor, in order to console the girl, gave her a necklace of black pearls with which Monsieur, the brother of Louis XIV, had once adorned himself. This gift did not solace Valérie; but in order not to displease her uncle, she dried her tears and three weeks later, in the chapel of the Tuileries, she married Prince Clément, who had been created King of Bramberg for the occasion. On their wedding night, when the young couple found themselves alone together, in the apartment which had been furnished for them in the Château de Saint-Cloud, the new Queen threw herself at her husband's feet and confessed, sobbing, that she did not love him. The King raised her from this position and admitted that in truth he did not love her either, for he intended to remain faithful to the unforgettable mem-

3

ory of the Countess Georgina de Solms, whom he would no doubt never see again. The night was spent in confidences, watered on either side with abundant tears. A reciprocal esteem, accompanied by a certain admiration, was the fruit of this curious conjugal situation. As the years passed, the Sovereigns of Bramberg presented the world an example of a couple united by mutual sacrifice, until the world wearied of admiring and gradually forgot them.

Such oblivion permitted them to escape the effects of the revision which the map of Europe suffered upon Napoleon's defeat. The Queen's position was not diminished by this event. Since she had given no heirs to the throne, the collateral branch of the Brambergs, assured of reigning eventually, had forgiven her for being the niece of the fallen tyrant. Doting on literature, on art and on music, she delighted to gather around herself the most eminent minds of the realm, but her chief concern was her people's happiness; and her husband, animated by the same sentiments, assisted her without stint in this task. There was no poverty which, once they learned of it, was not immediately succoured, no misfortune which failed to receive some assuagement, no despair which they did not attempt to remedy. To provide funds for their countless charities, the Sovereigns delved so deeply into their civil list that they were frequently obliged to reduce their personal expenditures. The King often observed that he was reluctant to order a new coat so long as a single one of his subjects was not suitably dressed, and the Queen gave her gowns away before she had worn them. Life at the Court was consequently of a simplicity which the nobility found frequent occasion to disparage: no parties, never balls, a few banquets on great occasions. There were no more military parades—why tire the men and the horses to no purpose?—no public executions, for the death penalty had been abolished. From time to time Queen Valérie invited several friends to a private concert. This was the only pleasure she permitted herself without remorse. If the weather was fine, the company sat on the terrace of the Royal Palace and the townspeople could contemplate at leisure, behind the gates, the diversions of Their Majesties. Several footmen in everyday livery handed round glasses of gooseberry wine; the Queen's ladies-in-waiting passed trays of cakes they had prepared with their own hands. On occasion the niece of Napoleon would sit down at the harpsichord and sing ballads whose subject never varied: it was ever a question of vanished love, of broken vows, of young girls nostalgically peering into silver ponds to discover there the reflection of an illusory happiness. In her vacant hours the Queen embroidered cushions with affecting inscriptions which celebrated the sweetness of friendship or the heart's constancy. She also painted upon squares of silk allegories celebrating the charms of love and distributed these souvenirs to her entourage. Yet all these activities could not rid the Queen's mind of the image of the handsome Hussar, which never faded. She had learned of his death crossing the Beresina, and since that time had renounced all effort to please by her *toilette*, adopting sombre gowns that reflected the colours of her melancholy. Indeed, as time passed, regret for her broken dream spread and flourished within her, like an incurable sickness. Sometimes, during a casual ride through the countryside, the beauty of a landscape would afford her an emotion sharp enough to revive a fleeting pleasure. She would order the coachman to stop and, leaning on the arm of a lady-in-waiting, walk to the nearest farm or cottage in order to speak to its occupants. Dazzled by these fine ladies, the peasants made curtsey upon curtsey while their children stared wide-eyed at the carriage and the dogs bayed wildly. The Queen engaged her subjects in conversation, eager to know if happiness was to be found here in this calm and rustic life, surrounded by an admirable nature. Were they happy? she asked anxiously. Alas, they never were! Aware of the Sovereign's proverbial kindness, her peasants never failed to bemoan at length their wretched lot. They paid little heed to a nature they had no leisure to contemplate. The Queen would return to her carriage and her palace, distressed by what she had heard, and the next day send some form of sustenance to these poor people.

Little by little Queen Valérie suffered the fate of all well-intentioned souls. She was exploited, betrayed, ignored. Accustomed to her kindnesses, the people no longer received them save with indifference. Families she had rescued from misery were the first to murmur at the parsimony of the Court and to reproach the Sovereigns' lack of pomp. A young officer whose gambling debts she had paid was implicated in a conspiracy and condemned to perpetual imprisonment. She solicited his pardon, obtained it, and was thanked for her intervention by a series of odious pamphlets the young man penned against his benefactress. Chance made itself the accomplice of human ingratitude. A female orphan she had undertaken to educate died at the age of eighteen, thereby depriving her of one of her fondest attachments. A child prodigy to whom she had given instructors abandoned his studies to keep his father's shop. The painter whose talent she had encouraged abandoned her Court to seek his fortune abroad, and the poet who had dedicated his verses to her hanged himself in the attic where she had gone to visit him one day that he was sick.

These successive failures had engendered in Queen Valérie a profound melancholy which, if it added a certain charm to her face, diminished that of her conversation. Her black eyes gleamed with secret tears, her complexion grew paler than ever, yet she remained lovely despite the ageing of her heart. She had gradually come to renounce all her habitual occupations, in order to shut herself up in her music room, where she remained closeted for whole days at a time, desiring no other company than that of an old blind dog that wandered through the room, occasionally knocking its head against the harp-strings and making them echo with a few plaintive tones.

The King showed himself all the more affected by his wife's

mysterious languor for feeling, on his side, that disenchantment compact of impotence and resignation which any man suffers whose no single aspiration has ever been realized. He knew that his name would remain in the history of Bramberg until the end of time and that posterity would perhaps be grateful to him for the sacrifice he had made to save his country, but this thought was not enough to satisfy him. What did the commemorative monuments matter to him, the equestrian statues, the medals with his effigy upon them and the squares to which his name had been given? He had never known that perfect felicity of which he used to dream in the days of his betrothal to the Countess Georgina, and he knew that it was now too late to find it ever again. He had the painful impression that a sheet of glass separated him from the external world and permitted him to observe the spectacle of life without taking part in it himself. Power lost all its value in his eyes, since he could not employ it to acquire the smallest part of that human reality in which the least of his subjects appeared to delight. The sadness which weighed upon his heart made him regret all the more sharply that he could not engage in the popular fêtes that frequently enlivened the low neighbourhoods of the capital. The children in the streets cruelly reminded him of those the Queen had never given him. Each being, each object was transformed for him into a pretext for bitter melancholy. An officer of his guard, hurrying to carry out his orders, transported him to the time of his youth when he had been an *aide-de-camp* of the Emperor Napoleon. A girl he had merely glimpsed revived in him the image of the Countess Georgina de Solms, whose memory became an obsession. She had died long since, after having married a Muscovite Prince, who beat her. At the thought of the sufferings the unfortunate creature had endured in that remote and barbarous Russia, he felt his love for her quicken feverishly. Why had he sacrificed her to the Emperor's wishes and his own father's ambition? At times he thought of abdicating and seeking asylum in some solitary place where he would wait for death, but his duty, in which he had never been remiss, kept him beside the Queen whose condition filled him with profound anxiety. Forty years of life together had strengthened the link of esteem and confidence which had been established between them on their wedding night, and they continued to admire, for lack of the power to love, each other.

One afternoon, the King, dressed as a simple citizen in a blue frock coat, was strolling, cane in hand, down the PrinzLuitpold-Strasse, when his attention was attracted by a crowd gathered before a house of modest appearance.

"What is going on here, my friend? Has someone been murdered?" he inquired of one of the loiterers.

"No, Your Majesty," answered the man, who had recognized him, "it is only a maker of automatons who is giving an exhibition."

The King expressed his curiosity to attend, and his interlocutor hastened to clear a path for him to the little room where the automatons were performing for some twenty persons. Their owner, to judge by his accent, was a foreigner; he had an honest countenance, a diligent expression. It was marvellous how he busied himself over his mechanical dolls, winding up their springs, pushing buttons, pulling pegs, regulating clockwork movements, and all this while giving copious explanations about his mechanisms. The King was thus able to learn that it had required four years to construct them and that each of them was able to write the same letter in five different languages. In truth, the crude way in which their wax faces were painted permitted them only a somewhat grotesque resemblance to human beings, yet the King was no less impressed, for all that, by the astonishing skill of the machinery which permitted the automatons' movements to retain all their suppleness without diminishing their precision. He read several times over the tiny square of paper on which one of the dolls had written: "I was constructed in Neuchâtel by the Sieur

Hans Brillaz, clockmaker", and asked for several portraits of the King of Prussia which the other automaton was drawing. Noticing the interest this visitor showed in his work, the Sieur Brillaz gladly repeated his demonstrations and ended by telling him that he had undertaken the construction of a third doll capable of playing a dozen different tunes upon the harpsichord.

The next day, at the first show of the afternoon, the Sovereign was again to be seen in the tiny room which served as a theatre for these ingenious marionettes. His enthusiasm was as great as it had been the day before, and, upon taking his leave, he invited the young clockmaker to appear that same evening at the palace to present his automatons to the Queen, who was very eager to see them. At the appointed hour a royal coach came to carry them there, and four footmen, with infinite precautions, bore the dolls to the Queen's chamber. Her husband had supposed that this spectacle would distract her, however briefly, from her ennui, and the pleasure which she took in them exceeded his every hope. For not only did the Queen not weary of seeing the automatons repeat the same movements all evening long, but she could not bear to have them taken away and offered to buy them on the spot. Their owner respectfully gainsaid this request, alleging that these machines were his only means of support and that if he sold them he would be obliged to ask in return a considerable sum in order that he could live without material cares during the entire period necessary to construct other examples. This refusal saddened the Queen, until she conceived an idea which she immediately expressed with unaccustomed vivacity:

"Why should we not suggest to this fine lad that he establish himself here in the palace, where we shall give him all he can require for his work?"

The King approved this offer, and specified the details of its conditions:

"You will receive a pension of five hundred florins a year,

and you will have no other task than to execute the Queen's commissions. . . ."

Delighted by this proposal, which assured his hitherto uncertain fate, and settled for a time his erstwhile vagabond life, Hans Brillaz eagerly accepted it. Several days later he took possession of a small apartment under the eaves of the palace. Waiting until the tools of which he had need arrived, he began to draw the plans for the two automatons which the Sovereigns had commissioned. These new dolls were to be even more extraordinary than the first pair. In every point similar to the human bodies whose dimensions they would have, they would lack, indeed, only the power of speech in order for the illusion to be complete. Hans Brillaz set to work with an ardour that stimulated the Queen's impatience. Day after day she spent long hours in the workshop of the young Swiss, watching him at work, leaning over his draughting table. The King was obliged to summon her in order to tear her from this fascinated contemplation. Spiteful tongues insinuated that she was in love with the artisan, but here they were mistaken, for the Queen thought only of the Hussar of her youth, whom she had decided to recall to life in the strangest manner that can be conceived. Hans Brillaz was for her only the instrument of this resurrection. She confided her project to the King.

"Why should I not do the same thing for the Countess Georgina?" he exclaimed, and both Sovereigns, delighted by this extravagant prospect, agreed to give to these new dolls the features of the beings they had loved and lost.

The construction of the two mechanisms lasted well over a year, during which the King abandoned the cares of government to concern himself with the automatons. He had put at the disposal of the Swiss the ten best clockmakers in his kingdom, and the latter had constructed the eight thousand seven hundred and fifty-three parts called for in the plans. On the day when a first attempt could be effected, his joy no longer knew any bounds. In Court and capital alike, there was talk of nothing but the marvellous machines, and everyone longed to see them, though the King had forbidden them to be shown before they were completed. A disciple of Madame Tussaud's came expressly from London to mould the bodies and to adapt their faces. The first models did not give satisfaction to the royal couple, who demanded many retouches. At least twenty times the operation was begun afresh but the result was never what was desired. The King criticized the colour of the wax; the Queen deplored the fact that the hinges of the fingers could not be concealed.

"It doesn't look at all like a real person," they both repeated, making no attempt to conceal their disappointment.

At the end of his patience, Madame Tussaud's pupil respectfully pointed out to Their Majesties that short of covering the figures with human skin it was impossible to give wax the aspect of epidermis.

These words served to furnish a flash of inspiration to the Sovereigns.

"What we need is the skin of a man and the skin of a woman!" exclaimed the kind and charitable Queen Valérie, who supposed that such a thing must be as easy to procure as the fur of a cat or a rabbit.

The Englishman stared at her, horror-struck.

"Your Majesty is not seriously thinking of such a thing!"

"Certainly," she replied. "I have heard that during the great revolution in France some people had the books of their libraries bound with the skins of guillotined aristocrats. It is reputed to be extremely durable!"

Fearing, no doubt, to be flayed alive on the spot, the Englishman requested his passports that very evening and left Bramberg the following day.

The King summoned the Royal Physician in order to explain that he desired the skin of a man and of a woman, both young and well constituted, of good family if possible, for individuals of condition took greater care of their appearance than the others. The woman's skin should be dark, for Kirghiz blood had run in the Countess Georgina's veins. This unwonted request cast Doctor Emerius into great embarrassment.

"But where does Your Majesty expect me to find two persons disposed to die in order to give up their skins? All the money in the world would not persuade them to do such a thing! Perhaps I could inquire at the hospital if some . . ."

"Do no such thing! I want creatures in good health. It might be better to visit the prison. There must be two or three rascals there who would serve the purpose. . . ."

At this moment the Minister of Justice, Baron de Weckmuhl, had himself announced.

"I trust Your Majesty will be good enough to pardon me, but I have lately learned an important piece of news which I preferred to waste no time in communicating to you. My agents have just arrested, in a house in the lower part of town, Lieutenant Hugo von Klopt, who has secretly returned from abroad to foment a new conspiracy against Your Majesty's life. I am in possession of the list of the conspirators and the details of their plot."

"It is heaven that sends you, my dear Baron!" the King exclaimed excitedly. "Have them all thrown in the dungeons and bring me the list you have secured."

The Minister withdrew.

"Truly there is a Providence!" the Monarch observed. "Doctor, you will have an embarrassment of riches from which to choose. Most of the conspirators must be young people of excellent family, spoilt by the foolish notions of liberalism circulating nowadays, and it would be devilish unlikely if you failed to discover among them a young woman to do us this little favour. . . . Ah! These traitors thought to assassinate me! It will cost them more than their lives. . . . The days of my clemency are past!"

He sent for the Queen, who entered the throne room just as the Baron de Weckmuhl returned.

"My dear, we have in our hands the two skins we needed! The Baron tells me that he has just arrested Lieutenant Hugo von Klopt, that young officer whose pardon you were kind enough to procure after his condemnation and who repaid your efforts by the blackest ingratitude. This time, there will be neither pardon nor banishment: he will be executed before the week is out. . . . Now let us consider the names of his accomplices. . . . Aha! What was I saying? Members of my nobility! Singular aberration. . . . What could they hope to obtain by my death? Oho! Ladies too. . . . The Countess Ludovine de Graben. . . . No, she has a hump. . . . Mademoiselle de Roon. . . . No, she is too short! The Baroness Ulrique de Sternow. . . . Splendid! A penniless girl to whom we gave a dowry, and now she decides to conspire against us! What was her part in this affair?"

"A modest one, Sire. She prepared meals for the conspirators when they forgathered in that house in the lower part of the capital."

"I hope she hasn't ruined her hands," the Queen murmured scornfully.

"You will see to the matter, Doctor Emerius," the Sovereign recommended. "Go visit the prisoners in their cells and make your preparations. A special commission will judge them all the day after tomorrow. The Lieutenant and the Baroness will be condemned to death and put at your disposal."

"But has Your Majesty, in his kindness, not suppressed the death penalty?" ventured the Baron de Weckmuhl.

"Re-establish it, then! I shall sign the decree tonight!" replied the Monarch, dismissing his Physician and his Minister.

Three days later Doctor Emerius proceeded with the flaying of the two corpses. The revelation of a murderous plot against the Sovereign had produced such great indignation throughout the kingdom that no one was surprised at the severity of the repression which ensued. The families of the condemned victims asked in vain for their bodies, which were buried in the prison courtyard. The skins underwent a suitable preparation which preserved their freshness and flexibility while at the same time rendering them imputrescible, and the automatons were covered with them. During this delicate operation a cat which had been prowling across the palace roofs slipped into the workshop through an open window and devoured a strip of flesh belonging to the late Baroness Ulrique de Sternow. The King fell into a great fit of rage when he was apprised of this unfortunate incident, and was appeased only by Doctor Emerius' promise to find another piece of skin.

"How will you manage?" groaned the King. "All my subjects are so blond, their skins are so pale! The Baroness de Sternow had no equal! And her flesh was so tender. . . ."

But the Physician kept his word, and the next morning he produced a square of brown, fine-grained, rather shiny skin which won the old Sovereign's admiration forthwith.

"Where did you ever manage to cut it from?" he inquired.

"In Your Majesty's forests there are caravans of Bohemians, and after the manner of their kind these gypsies do not know just how many children they have. . . ." answered the Physician, his tone somewhat abashed.

The King dared not insist, and contented himself with having his Chaplain say a Requiem Mass for a special intention.

The creation of the wigs was a charming pastime for Queen Valérie. A serving-girl renowned for her splendid hair was ordered to cut it off. The younger brother of the King's Huntsman received a command to shave his black locks that had made him a modern Antinous. The Court Barber assisted the Queen in dressing the wigs on the automatons. In Vienna, the dressmaker of the Archduchess Sophie created a series of gowns, all faithful copies of those worn in the days of the Countess Georgina. From Paris, a former General of the Imperial Armies brought a Hussar's uniform that conformed in every detail to the regulations of the year 1806.

The ceremony adopted for the first demonstration of the automatons was that of the formal presentations at Court in the last years of the eighteenth century. Forgotten pomp was revived for the occasion. After a banquet of twelve hundred covers in the Grand Gallery of the palace, the Formal Salons, long since closed, were opened once again to receive a considerable crowd of nobles and sensation-seekers who had come from the four corners of the realm. The Sovereigns, sumptuously arrayed, assumed their thrones, and, in an awesome silence, the Grand Master of Ceremonies announced the entrance of the automatons. A door opened at the end of the room; an heroic fanfare—the March of the Bercheny Hussars—was heard; and to the general stupefaction two persons as real as those who were staring at them appeared upon the threshold: an officer and a young girl, holding one another's hand and smiling graciously to the throng. They remained motionless for several seconds, and all could see the young man's heart beating under his dolman, the throat of his companion fluttering above the generous *décolleté* of her gown. Their eyes wandered over the crowd as though looking for someone, and then those standing closest heard the sound of a faint click and the automatons, though neither supported nor led, made for the two thrones. At this moment a terrible shriek drowned out the murmurs that were beginning to fill the hall:

"My daughter! It is my daughter!"

A woman dressed in black attempted to fling herself towards the automatons, but two gentlemen-in-waiting restrained her and immediately held a handkerchief over her mouth to stifle her cries. It was the mother of the Baroness Ulrique de Sternow, whom a kind of premonition had brought to the palace that day. She was taken away half mad with grief. That evening she was entirely so. The next day she was dead.

This interruption had produced no effect upon the automatons, who, having arrived within several feet of the Sovereigns, suddenly stopped. The officer saluted; the girl curtseyed and then sat down at a harpsichord, where she played a tune composed long ago by the Queen. Leaning against the instrument, the officer turned the pages of the music. The public did not wait for the end of the melody to manifest its astonishment by frenzied applause. It was necessary to have the automatons make their entrance several times over, and on each occasion their inventor contrived to have them play different tunes, but all products of Queen Valérie's talent. That evening, exhausted by the day's emotions and the recollections which these creatures of illusion had revived, the King and the Queen fell into one another's arms, weeping for joy. They had found happiness at last.

From this moment on, the most singular follies marked the reign of a Monarch hitherto renowned for the enlightened wisdom of his authority. A royal decree of October 15, 1846, created the automatons Prince and Princess de Landermuhlen, a title formerly attached to an extinct branch of the House of Bramberg, and each doll had its own house with a major-domo, chamberlains, grooms, and ladies-in-waiting. Some months after the ceremony of their presentation at Court, Queen Valérie conceived the idea of celebrating their marriage. The Bishop of Bramberg having refused to lend his support to this sacrilegious masquerade, he was deposed and, despite the Vatican's opposition, replaced by a less scrupulous young Abbé, who complied with the Sovereigns' every preference. This measure provoked the displeasure of the clergy, which was soon swelled by that of the people, oppressed as the latter were by new and excessive taxes. Indeed the Sovereigns, considering their palace unworthy of the automatons, had decided to build for them a fantastical residence which was to exceed the Belvedere in splendour, the Royal Pavilion at Brighton in originality. None of the projects which his Royal Architect submitted having pleased him, the King appealed, for the creation of this supreme architectural achievement, to the Austrian master Arnold Reyniff, who designed the plans for a palace such as might have been conceived by a Sultan of the *Thousand and One Nights*. The construction was immediately begun. To make room for this sublime edifice, two convents were demolished, and to improve the view from its windows the hospital was razed which the King had constructed on the site early in his reign. The expenses of these labours wrought such disorder in the Royal Exchequer that it became necessary to resort to measures of expedience: loans were floated, gaming houses opened; the confiscations of estates multiplied; on the other hand, pensions of old soldiers, invalids and widows were suppressed. Peaceful Bramberg began to live in terror. The automatons had bewitched the Sovereigns, transformed their sentiments and altered their habits. Life in the palace was now nothing but a series of parties whose sole purpose was to set off to advantage the Prince and Princess of Landermuhlen. There were Persian balls, Chinese ridottos, Muscovite entertainments, on the occasion of which the new toys appeared in the most magnificent garb. The evenings at the Opera became brilliant, for the automatons attended them in the first row of the Royal Box. The races at Krallein, which had hitherto been merely an equestrian exercise for the local nobility, soon rivalled in elegance those of Baden-Baden. There was a "Prince de Landermuhlen Prize" whose enormous purse attracted the finest horsemen of Europe. From all directions people hastened to see these prodigious mechanical phenomena, and the hotels were never empty. One day certain fanatics managed to deceive the vigilance of the police and fired upon the gala coach that was carrying the Prince and Princess to the theatre. The Prince was quite seriously wounded in the peg forming the joint of his right arm. A dozen executions avenged this assault.

The Chancelleries of the Courts of Europe were properly amazed at this singular whim, which now was assuming dangerous proportions. The Ambassador of Her Majesty the Queen of England had been dismissed for refusing to pay court to the Princess, and the Minister Plenipotentiary of the King of Sweden had found himself forbidden access to the palace on the pretext that the Prince de Landermuhlen did not enjoy his company. Domestically, the collateral branch of the Princes of Bramberg saw its rights to the throne threatened by the King's intention to name the Prince as his successor. The Sovereign announced to his entourage, moreover, that the clockmaker of Neuchâtel was constructing a young Heir Apparent and that the dynasty's future was consequently assured. When this last news was heard in Vienna, the Emperor immediately sent two regiments which, without firing a shot, occupied the entire kingdom. The King was obliged to abdicate and was confined, along with the Queen, in the Château de Mackenwirt. Their departure from the palace gave rise to an agonizing scene, for authorization to take the automatons with them had been refused. The niece of Napoleon burst into sobs and dejectedly embraced the Prince of Landermuhlen, whose skin stretched slightly under the tears of his disconsolate beloved. The King clung to the Princess's gown with such energy that the Austrian officer responsible for escorting him to his seclusion was obliged to have his men carry him off bodily. Their cries long rent the lugubrious silence of the Château de Mackenwirt, an ancient fortress abandoned since the Thirty Years' War. Mattresses were placed against the walls to prevent the royal pair from breaking open their heads. The King died after several months, in a state close to madness. The Queen survived him by a number of years. She had recovered her calm, if not her spirits, and spent her days copying out ballads which she afterwards flung from the window of her bedroom.

Upon the accession of Prince Sigismond, head of the collateral branch, Hans Brillaz was dismissed and asked permission to take with him the automatons which represented his only fortune. He exhibited them throughout the world and finally sold them to a collector who passed them on to another admirer of curiosities. At the end of the nineteenth century the Princess de Landermuhlen, though somewhat the worse for wear, was acquired by the Khedive of Egypt, who placed her in his harem, where his wives took the greatest possible care of her.

The Prince's destiny was more mysterious. He belonged for a time to the Marquis de Custine, who bequeathed him to his friend Monsieur de Foudras. Upon the latter's death, the image of the handsome Hussar was put up for auction at Christie's, in London, where it brought the fabulous sum of three thousand pounds sterling and became the property of Lady Edwina Weresdale, wife of an attaché at the English Embassy in Saint Petersburg. It is said that the automaton was stolen from her there by the old Countess Zacheroff and that it disappeared in the looting of the Zacheroff Palace in 1917.

The Margravine's Page

■ ■ ■ In order to render an eternal homage to beauty and ■ ■ ■
youth alike, a Margravine of Breitenstadt, greedy until her last
hour for pretty boys, had instituted a singular competition,
and in her will had scrupulously decreed its details: each year,
thirty students of the University, selected from among those
who were the handsomest and most well made, gathered together for a great banquet, at the termination of which they
designated the one of their number who seemed to them most
worthy of receiving the prize of ten thousand thalers established by the Sovereign. The victor was borne in triumph
through the streets of the city, then the Court Painter limned
his portrait. If he were a foreigner, he received letters of natu-
ralization; if he were not of noble blood, he became so. Further, his studies were subsidized until their completion, out of
the Margrave's privy purse.

This institution enjoyed a great vogue among the students,
who had rebelled when the Margrave Theodore had attempted to abolish it. Nonetheless its principal attraction did
not reside in the material advantages or the satisfactions of
vanity which it afforded. By a clause of her testament, the
lovesick old lady had provided that the fortunate laureate
would be invited to spend his vacation with the Court, and this
honour, for those who knew how to exploit it, became in most
cases the point of departure of a brilliant career. Consequently
the famous contest excited the ambitions of all, and ardent ri-
valries resulted from it, which were occasionally terminated by
moonlight duels upon the ramparts.

In this year of 1813 it appeared that the election would pro-

voke no difficulties, for even before being officially awarded the prize fell by rights to a certain young student, Carl Tieborg. He had arrived from Sweden some months earlier, and his beauty had produced a profound emotion of which he appeared to be unaware. He was a slender creature, his face still beardless. His clear Northern colouring gave the pure and delicate lines of his countenance a marvellous seductive power. There was such perfection in his features that even the coarsest observer could not fail to be affected by them, and the former Prince-Bishop of Basle, who had one day come to visit the University, exclaimed upon seeing him: "What an admirable symbol of Celestial Eternity!"

Expert at every bodily exercise, Carl Tieborg was less brilliant in those of the mind, and rarely participated in the noisy discussions of which his comrades were so fond. He loved solitude, and made long excursions into the surrounding countryside; from them he returned deliciously weary, his cheeks scarlet and his lips half-open in a faint smile. His presence in the city had troubled the most innocent hearts, awakened passions that had been extinguished, and agitated the most obscure desires. A girl of fifteen, to whom he had never spoken a word, had thrown herself down a well in despair. An ancient member of the Aulic Council, wakened from his senility, ordered his coach and four to be taken out every day in order to see the youth leave the University gates, then returned to his residence, shivering with ague on the cushions of the vehicle's curtained depths. The Burgomaster's wife, a lady as voracious as she was mature, had retired to an abbey in order to escape a temptation to which the young Swede's indifference did not allow her to succumb. On the other hand, a novice in attendance at a convent turnbox, having glimpsed Carl through the grille of her lodge, had fallen so wildly in love with him that she had been unable to bring herself to pronounce her vows. She had abandoned the veil and taken up residence in a modest family *pension* opposite the student's lodgings, where she anxiously

spied on his comings and goings. Some wretched embroidery work, which society ladies purchased from her out of curiosity to hear her story, gained her a meagre livelihood.

At the University itself, Carl scored no fewer successes, but hitherto he had showed to none of his admirers a predilection susceptible of being interpreted as an avowal.

The competition this year was therefore nothing but a mere formality, and at the end of the traditional banquet Carl Tieborg, by universal acclamation, found himself elected the handsomest boy that the University had ever counted upon its benches. Enthusiastic toasts were drunk to his honour, and many of his friends sought oblivion of their sentimental disappointments in intoxication. The ceremony was terminated by a memorable orgy, in which Carl took no part. At dawn he slipped out of the hall and returned to his apartment. The former lay-sister was spying on him from behind her curtains, and the Aulic Councillor's equipage had stopped several yards away from his door.

Fifteen days later, the Court left the palace for the Château of Kaummertzau, where Margravine Frederica had decided to spend the summer, in her husband's absence. This latter, after having fought in the Russian campaign at the Emperor Napoleon's side, had remained loyal to him in the hopes of being created a Grand Duke, which was the ambition of his life. At the head of a regiment recruited upon his domains, he was waging war somewhere in Germany and rarely sent news to his Court. The Margravine consoled herself by taking part in various intrigues which mingled politics and love in such wise that she had considerable difficulty in distinguishing them. Consequently she was delighted to leave Breitenstadt for several months in order to seek repose from the responsibilities of the Regency. She left with a small suite composed of only some ten persons. The Dowager Margravine, who had retired to Kaummertzau since her son's accession to the throne, had a sufficiently numerous household to permit the Reigning

Margravine to dispense with bringing her own. Carl Tieborg would be her distraction for the summer, and as she drove at good speed along the road to Kaummertzau she mused with pleasure upon the charming youth who had been presented to her the day after the competition. He was travelling with the Major-Domo, but at the first relay of horses the Margravine sent her Lady-in-Waiting to join the Major-Domo in his carriage and took Carl in hers. She admired his face, which she could not keep from gazing at continually.

The Dowager Margravine, who had fallen into pious ways, promptly recovered her secular self at the sight of the handsome Swede. She was soon quarrelling over him with her daughter-in-law, and for his sake began to neglect her erstwhile favourite, an Austrian Jesuit in the pay of the Viennese Court. The Major-Domo, who had been the old Margravine's lover some forty years before, experienced anew the torments of a jealous heart and suffered from them all the more sharply in that he was not insensitive to the young foreigner's charms. The latter, nonetheless, remained as distant and detached as he had ever been in Breitenstadt. The only object for which he had shown some interest was the portrait of the reigning Margrave, Christian VII, a magnificent canvas executed by David during one of the model's sojourns in Paris. Christian VII, in order to flatter the Emperor, had had himself represented in the uniform of a French General, whose sobriety emphasized the elegance of his figure, but what was most remarkable about this painting was the expression of the face, which the artist had rendered to perfection. The young Margrave passed for the handsomest man of his country, though he was not of the national type. From his mother, a Roman princess, he had inherited an antique profile tempered by a certain softness about the lines of the mouth, illuminated by a gaze in which might be divined a noble and secret melancholy. The first time he had seen it, Carl had stood for a long time staring at this painting, and thereafter lost no occasion to cast frequent glances at it each time he went to pay his court to the Dowager Margravine, for the canvas happened to hang in her boudoir. No one divined the purport of this interest, and the two Margravines attributed it the one to love of the dynasty, the other to love of art. In reality, the charming Swede, for the first time in his life, was, quite simply, in love, although he had three reasons not to be so: was it not madness to love an image, particularly if it was that of a man, and of a Prince whom everything separated from him? He dissimulated his passion, but lived still more at a remove from the little Court, a fact which greatly distressed the two Sovereigns. He spent the greater part of his days in the forest, walking where his humour led him, his mind entirely occupied by Christian VII, and returned only at nightfall, exhausted and still more melancholy than he had been by day.

One afternoon in the month of August the heat was so oppressive that he had renounced his forest wanderings in order to sit upon the bank of the Lake of Warsee, some half a league from the château, so as to enjoy the cool of the spot. He had remained for a moment observing the shifting reflection of the clouds upon the mirror of the water, then, gradually, he had fallen asleep. A sound of footsteps roused him from his somnolence, and he observed before him a young boy approaching his resting-place without appearing to see him. He was holding in his hands a pair of ice skates, but what astonished Carl even more was the curious costume he was wearing: a kind of green velvet doublet, richly embroidered and festooned, with a carefully starched ruff. On his head he wore a bonnet that matched the doublet and sported a white feather. He stopped a few feet away from Carl, whose presence he still did not appear to notice, sat down upon the grass, then bent forward slightly in order to fasten his skates. Carl's stupefaction was so great that he did not dare to move. This boy was entirely unknown to him, and he dismissed the notion that he might have been watching some young servant from the château. Why would the latter have been so bizarrely dressed, and where would he have obtained such a costume in the first place? The stranger finished attaching the clasps of his skates, then slipped down the bank and remained, hesitating for a moment, his legs dangling over the water. At the moment when Carl was about to intervene, he straightened up and sped out upon the lake, whose surface miraculously sustained him. Such a prodigy confounded the young Swede, who desired to warn the skater of the danger he was running, but a strange numbness prevented him from making the least gesture or from uttering a single word. For how long did he watch, or believe he watched, the skater perform his circuit of the lake and execute thereupon various acrobatic arabesques? His anxiety afforded him, of the seconds as of the minutes, an inexact measurement, which did not permit any estimate of the duration of this extraordinary spectacle. Suddenly the image grew dim and gradually faded away. Carl, emerging from his torpor, straightened up and examined the spot where the boy had been sitting upon the bank. The grass retained no trace of his footsteps. Convinced he had been the dupe of a dream, he returned to the château and breathed no word of this adventure to anyone.

The next day, however, as soon as he could make his escape from the Dowager Margravine's salon, where she had begun to dictate her memoirs to him, he returned to the shores of the lake and sat down in the same place as the day before. The weather was fine, but the heat less intense, and he resisted sleep more easily. Once his attention was distracted by a vulture soaring over the water, and he followed it with his eyes until it had disappeared in the forest. When he looked back at the shore, he had a moment of alarm upon seeing that the young skater was there again, a few yards away from him, and unaware of his presence. He attempted to stand, but, as on the foregoing day, a mysterious force held him fast to the ground and rendered him mute. He watched, powerless, the repetition of the scene he had already witnessed. The boy slid down to the edge of the water, tested the surface with the tip of his foot, then hurled himself forward, bold, light, heedless, the white plume in the wind, his arms raised toward the sky. Carl watched him, fascinated. All of a sudden he heard a cracking noise: the ice had just broken.

"Look out! Look out!" he shrieked.

In his consternation, he had forgotten his German and employed his mother tongue. He was about to rush to the daring stranger's rescue, but the vision disappeared. The water was calm, without ripples, and the shadows of the clouds were anchored upon it, motionless. This time he was certain he had not dreamed, and, his mind profoundly disturbed, he returned in haste to the château in order to describe this fantastic scene.

The two Sovereigns were sitting on the terrace. The Major-Domo was reading them the verses of Herr von Goethe, while the Lady-in-Waiting was executing a watercolour. All broke off what they were doing upon seeing Carl's agitation.

"What is the matter, my dear child?" the Dowager Margravine inquired, her voice more maternal than the hand that stroked her new favourite's blond locks.

"I trust Your Most Serene Highness will deign to excuse the liberty I am taking, but I have been the witness of a scene so bizarre that unless I have been the toy of my own imagination . . . it is not possible for me to explain it."

Nonetheless, he undertook to tell his story, but upon the first words the Dowager Margravine fainted, dropping her teacup and scalding the pug that had been lying on her knees. The animal's cries were echoed by those of the young Margravine, while the Lady-in-Waiting and the Major-Domo repeated with consternation:

"He has seen the Sign. . . . He has seen the Sign!"

Lackeys appeared, then the Court Physician and the Jesuit Father, who in his alarm gave absolution to everyone. The Dowager Margravine came to herself after a few moments.

The young Dowager controlled herself, wept a little. They asked to be left alone with Carl and, in their turn, explained to him the cause of their emotion. It was a tradition among the Margraves of Breitenstadt that the death of each of them was always announced by the apparition of the young skater of Warsee. Three centuries before, Dorothée de Breitenstadt had expressed for one of her husband's pages an inclination which was not at all compatible with the elevation of her rank and the rigour of manners in those days. Although he took umbrage at the affair, the husband of Margravine Dorothée would not have dreamed of ridding himself of his young rival by a crime, and merely intended to exile the lad from his Court, when chance forestalled his decision.

One winter afternoon, the handsome page, who had gone skating with several friends upon the Lake of Warsee, ventured too far and suddenly vanished, uttering a great cry of distress. The ice, too thin in the centre of the lake, had broken under his weight and his friends arrived too late to save him. Dorothée de Breitenstadt proved an inconsolable mistress, and her husband, who was a sensitive soul, shared her grief. Both Sovereigns erected a splendid mausoleum for the unfortunate youth. In gratitude, apparently, the page assumed the habit of coming to skate upon the lake each time that the mortal term of a Margrave was close at hand. This was a presage by which no one could be deceived; the life of Christian VII was certainly in danger, had perhaps even ceased. His mother and his wife spent the following days in the cruellest anxiety, and Carl, to whom the Sovereign was no less dear, partook of their grief. Since nothing had as yet confirmed the sad news, the Court had not gone into mourning, but its grief was nevertheless evident on every face, and in every heart.

One week later, an *estafette* of the Imperial Army appeared while the two Margravines, sitting as usual on the terrace, were staring down the avenue in hopes of sighting a courier. Both fainted upon seeing that the man was waving a letter. The

Major-Domo seized and opened the missive with respect, for he had recognized the Emperor's seal. In fact, this latter wrote in his own hand to announce that, thanks to the courage of the Margrave Christian de Breitenstadt and to the heroic defence of his grenadiers, the Empire had won the Battle of Märtzen. The Margrave had received a slight wound in the fray, but he would recover swiftly and soon return to reassure his family and his subjects as to his fate.

The château was illuminated and couriers were dispatched to Breitenstadt in order to spread the happy news there. The two Margravines could not read the imperial missive often enough and never wearied of discussing it, when all of a sudden the Dowager Margravine moaned and fainted away once again. No sooner had she recovered her senses than she held out the letter to her daughter-in-law, pointing to the date: it was anterior to Carl's vision. . . . The Battle of Märtzen was not the danger which the Margrave had incurred. Another, much more serious, had occurred, which he had doubtless not escaped. Tears drowned the candles and new couriers were sent out to recall the first.

At the end of the month of August, as the Emperor's letter had announced, Christian VII, still convalescent, returned to Kaummertzau. When the emotion provoked by this unhoped-for return had somewhat abated, he gave, upon widespread request, an account of his adventures. He had indeed received a flesh wound at the Battle of Märtzen, and that very evening he had gone to be cared for by the Emperor's own surgeon, who had set up his hospital in a nearby château. The extraction of the bullet caused him to bleed copiously. Greatly weakened, he had had to remain at the château for several days in order to recover his strength. One afternoon, while he was dozing on his bed, he suddenly had the sense of an inhabitual presence. He opened his eyes, and to his great alarm saw the head of a Cossack leaning towards him, through the open window. His stupor left him speechless and deprived him of any reflex of

defence. The château must have been unexpectedly surrounded by the enemy, but how did it happen that no one had
as yet given the alarm? Had all the occupants been already
slaughtered, as he now would be, without having had time to
commend their souls to God? The soldier unsheathed his
sabre and prepared to leap through the window. The Margrave, paralysed by terror, attempted to cry out, but his voice
stuck in his throat. At that moment he heard someone shouting twice over a word he did not understand. The Cossack,
surprised, hesitated, then fled. Soon a tumult of arms, and several shots, followed by a noise of galloping hoofs, shattered the
silence. The troop of Russian horsemen who had attempted to
seize the château by surprise was rapidly dispersed. With the
exception of an old commander, who, wakened suddenly, had
died of fear, there was no other loss to deplore in the episode.
Everyone was questioned in order to discover who had first
given the alarm, but no one was able to identify the voice. Only
an old soldier who had formerly served in Sweden produced
the notion that it must have been a Swede, for he had clearly
heard the words "Look out!" shouted twice over in that language. Despite all inquiries, no one was found besides this
man who spoke Swedish, and, in order not to let this incident
be shrouded in mystery, he was decorated forthwith.

The Margravines hastened to disclose the truth of the matter, and everyone gave himself up to amazement. Christian
VII summoned Carl Tieborg to question him. At the sight of
the young man, he grew strangely pale and in a trembling
voice requested him to tell his own story. Carl obeyed, with ill-
concealed emotion. His consternation was so great that the
Margrave recovered a little of his own *sang-froid*, but both of
them, with a single glance, had divined that the secret they
bore in their hearts was one and the same. This permitted
them to keep it more easily in sharing it. No one in the Court
suspected their liaison, which escaped the perspicacity of both
Margravines.

In October Christian VII was to set off for the wars once again. The campaign threatened to be a hard one, and the winter as well. The Court regained Breitenstadt, and the University once again opened its doors. Carl resumed his place there, but he was still more remote, more absent than the preceding year. He scarcely seemed alive at all, lost in some inner dream whose object none of his comrades could discern or divine.

One winter morning he wakened earlier than usual. He arose, dressed himself, put his affairs in order, took up his ice skates and left his apartment. No one saw him. The ancient Aulic Councillor had died a month before and the former nun, weary of watching from behind her curtains, had fallen asleep. He reached Warsee in the afternoon. The lake was imprisoned beneath a thick layer of ice, bristling here and there with tufts of aquatic weeds, now desiccated and yellow. He attached his skates and, as he had seen the page of Margravine Dorothée do the summer before, let himself slip down onto the glassy surface. For almost half an hour he circled with surprising agility before the delighted eyes of several young peasants who had emerged from nearby cottages to admire him.

Suddenly a terrible cracking sound rang out in the frozen air. The ice had just yielded and the young Swede vanished, uttering a great cry which was echoed by those of the young peasants. At the same moment, while crossing the Rhine at Mannheim, Christian VII, the last hereditary Margrave of Breitenstadt, had his head shot off by a cannonball.

The Force of Destiny

■ ■ ■ THE RAIN HAD BEEN FALLING for several hours with ■ ■ ■
such violence that the road from Graz to Léoben had become
a bog in which the carriages were bemired over the axle-trees.
Yet one of them continued to advance, its horses struggling
against the storm that flayed the trees and, by a just antithesis,
whipped the coachman swaying on his box. The wind had
blown out the lanterns, and in this May twilight that was
darker than a November midnight the berlin resembled a
hearse bearing the damned to Hell. Inside the carriage, its
owner, Count Adam de Stimmlicher, gave himself up to a profound melancholy. He had only his thoughts for company, and
these were the saddest that can be imagined. Two days before,
he had received the last breath of his third fiancée, Mademoiselle Adélaïde de Wabern, dead, like her predecessors, of a
strange languishing sickness against which all medical science
had proved to be impotent. The Count could not bear to be
present at the interment ceremonies: like one possessed, he had
fled the room without even speaking to the Baroness de Wabern, who was sobbing at the foot of her daughter's bed, and
he had determined to return at once to his own home in order
to bury his grief there.

Suddenly the equipage came to a stop. The coachman's
streaming face appeared in the frame of the window. Count
Adam lowered the glass and a gust of wind roared into the
carriage. The Count shivered.

"What is it, Hermann? Is the road washed out?"

"No, Your Excellency, but the horses are winded, and we
shall never reach Léoben this night. If Your Excellency is will-

ing, we could try to make Tauplitz, which should be only a quarter of a league from here. It would be better to spend the night there than on this cursed road. . . ."

Count Adam took pity on the man, who truly seemed to have reached the limit of his strength.

"Very well, Hermann! Drive us to the place. We shall wait there until the end of this tempest. . . ."

The team furnished a supreme effort, which brought the carriage into the courtyard of the "Angel Gabriel", Tauplitz's only inn at the time. Other travellers, surprised on their way by the bad weather, had already taken refuge here, and were dining gaily before a roaring fire. To avoid their noisy company, the young man requested the innkeeper's wife to have his dinner served in his room.

"In your room!" the latter exclaimed. "Alas! All my rooms are taken. I have had to give up even my own to a pair of foreign ladies who arrived a few moments before Your Lordship, and I have nothing else to offer you."

"Have you not at least another room where I might dine alone and rest a little: I am so weary. . . ."

"Ah! Your Lordship has no use for company!" exclaimed the coarse woman in a jolly tone. "But he must either put up with it this evening or go elsewhere."

Vexed by this vulgar joviality, Count Adam restrained a gesture of impatience and was about to give his man orders to set off again when his eyes met those of a man sitting at a small table in the darkest corner of the room. This person was finishing a solitary repast. His countenance was so strange that it was difficult to determine his age with any accuracy. Count Adam decided he was quite old. The simplicity of his attire indicated a person of modest station, though the elegance of his manners betrayed the man of the world. The elderly stranger must have overheard his dialogue with the innkeeper's wife, for he half rose to his feet and with a courteous gesture offered to share his table with the Count.

"Have no fear that I shall importune you with my conversation! I hold solitude too dear not to respect another man's. We shall keep silent on whatever subjects you like!"

Although astonished by the ironic tone in which this invitation was couched, the Count accepted it, sat down opposite the stranger and introduced himself.

"Permit me not to tell you my name," the old man replied. "It is a detail I have long since forgotten."

Count Adam regarded his *vis-à-vis* with an even more marked surprise. Was he a madman or a philosopher? Curious to discover which, the Count could not forbear to speak again.

"Now that is the most singular declaration I have ever heard! Is it possible to live without having a name?"

"You are quite right, but who is to say that I am alive?"

At these words Count Adam decided that he was certainly dealing with a madman, but since such extravagant conversation distracted him from his grief, he continued it. The old man intrigued him.

"I have always believed in ghosts," he said. "Are you one?"

"No, but I am dead. Later on, monsieur, you may boast, if you like, of having known a dead man. No one knows the dead. No sooner has a person ceased to breathe than he is hustled out of sight, buried underground the better to be rid of him. He is smothered beneath the weight of enormous stones; bushes are planted on his grave so that their roots may bind him and keep him from escaping. His goods are stripped from him, the rank he occupied is usurped, he is driven from the society to which he once belonged. Ah, what ignoble treatment! In my youth I believed I should never die: the world, in my eyes, was a vast but immutable tableau of which each element was fixed for eternity. There were old men whom I did not conceive to have been children, and children whom I did not suspect were capable of growing old. Oh, those years of illusion! They are the only ones we may truly be said to have lived, my dear Count. . . . The rest are as nothing beside them. They merely mark off the road that leads to our end. What is the use of enduring them at all?"

The stranger sank into his reflections and completed his dinner. Count Adam began his own. After a moment or so, he addressed himself to the stranger once again.

"You remarked a moment ago, monsieur, that you were dead. How did such an event occur?"

"Did I not just observe that a man's death deprived him of all he possessed: family, friends, fortune, social position?"

"Yes, it is a matter of evidence."

"And has it never occurred to you that the converse was true, and that by dissociating oneself from all such things one might consider oneself to be dead?"

"I fear I do not understand, monsieur."

"It is my turn to say to you: a matter of evidence! A dead man *is* nothing, *has* nothing. Therefore, if I abandon my position in the world and strip myself of all my goods . . . I am dead!"

The Count acknowledged himself vanquished by the logic of such reasoning, but declared himself curious to learn by what means the old man had put it into practice.

"I have renounced everything that constituted me a man of this world; I have separated myself from all that made me a son, a husband, a father or a lover; I have broken all the ties that bound me here on earth; I have freed myself from all the fetters that render the human condition so wretched yet are not strong enough to retard our flight into oblivion."

"What a horrible sacrifice!" murmured Count Adam, shocked in spite of himself. "How could you bring yourself to effect this determination?"

And, actuated by an impulse of sudden compassion, he added, with a tinge of respect in his voice:

"You must have suffered great misfortunes!"

The stranger produced a sneer:

"Great misfortunes! Alas, no! I suppose, rather, that they are precisely what I lacked, for one lives on one's misfortunes;

34

one comes, in the end, to expect them; one compares them in order to congratulate oneself on the fact that one of our ills is less terrible than another. . . . Never has this opportunity been granted to me, and it is for this reason that I have chosen to forestall the death which awaits me at the end of my earthly career. Can you not understand that there is as much joy in destroying as in creating, more pleasure in precipitating time's course than in trying to struggle in vain against it? Do you not realize that all must one day vanish, that each thing must return to the Void, and that all our efforts will never succeed in breaking this inexorable rule? Have you never conceived that all these objects which tonight surround us will already have disappeared tomorrow? Consider the flame of this candle, the wine in that carafe, the piece of bread beside your plate! What will be left of them in a few hours? You will no longer even remember them. The very beings dearest to us eventually return to nothingness and sink into oblivion. . . ."

"I shall never forget Mademoiselle Adélaïde de Wabern," her fiancé protested energetically.

"What did you say?"

"I said I shall never forget Mademoiselle de Wabern. We were promised to one another by the tenderest vows, and she died two days ago. . . ." he explained with a sob in his throat.

"Ah! My dear Count, how I envy you! How splendid to bear within oneself a melancholy of which one knows the cause! What a privilege to watch a creature one loves dying in the prime of life—for to judge by the signs of your grief, I am certain that you loved her. . . ."

At these words, Count Adam could not restrain his tears, which as they fell upon the candle made it gutter. He found some comfort in giving the old man an account of his sad adventures.

"Weep not," the latter declared when he had finished speaking. "Rather rejoice to have cause to be overwhelmed by your grief!"

"But if there were no cause for despair, there would be no

despair," returned the young man, whose sense of logic rebelled against this paradox. "Is this not always the case?"

"Would that what you said were true, my friend, but, alas,
there are beings who experience only the effects of passion and
bear upon their shoulders a burden of sadness of whose origin
they are forever unaware. You have shown me your confidence
by opening your heart to me; I shall prove mine to you by telling my story."

The other travellers had finished their dinners, and the two
were now alone in the tremendous, shadowy common-room.
Outside, the wind and the rain continued to rage, and for the
first time in two days Count Adam experienced a sensation of
relief which disposed him to listen to the old man's narrative
with the liveliest interest.

"I must say," the latter began, "that I have not always been
this species of vagabond who is dining opposite you this evening. I even enjoyed some reputation in foreign capitals. I
found, indeed, that it was not so hard to shine there, for everything concurred to make of me one of those favoured beings
who seem destined for the most extraordinary achievements. I
had the birth, the fortune and an intelligence which allowed
me to seek the highest posts in the Empire. I passed for handsome, I was admitted to have wit. All women loved me, some
exaggeratedly. What more could I hope for? All I lacked was
that spark which communicates enthusiasm, that mysterious
spring which animates the human machinery and causes it to
function without its being aware of doing so. Instead of sharing the exaltation of the young men my own age, I was overcome by a melancholy so profound that I could not take part in
a conversation without immediately perceiving its futility, nor
conceive any plan without divining that its realization was a
sterile activity of which, one day, nothing would remain. Indeed, I do not remember a period of my existence when I have
not suffered from this melancholy.

"At first as gentle as a spring mist, it enveloped my adolescence in an atmosphere whose subtle charm I enjoyed without realizing that it would become so noxious to me. As a child, in Vienna, I spent hours in the grounds of our mansion, watching the sun slip across the façade, obliquely illuminating the tall windows, then vanish, leaving me in despair without my being able to discover the reason for this despair. I dimly anticipated that my life would resemble one of those great dark rooms where the sun never shone. I was fifteen years old when my father was appointed Ambassador to King Ferdinand of Naples. One might suppose that the climate of Italy would produce a salutary effect upon my mind. Yet no such thing occurred. The pleasures of the Court distracted without occupying me. So much heedlessness and frivolity produced in me a sense of frustration which I could not explain. Indeed, had I known what I desired, I should have attempted the impossible to find it; but it was in vain that I questioned myself as I walked along the murmurous shore of the Mediterranean. My first experiences of love did not help me to resolve this problem. I made conquests which flattered my *amour-propre* but did not waken more ardent sentiments in my heart. It was at this point that I measured the whole extent of the ravages which this strange sickness of the soul had wrought upon me. One day, just as I was taking my mistress in my arms, I experienced a sensation of intense horror, as if I had clasped a corpse to my bosom. My anguish was so great that, without finding the strength to speak a word, I stood up and left her."

"What had happened?" asked Count Adam.

"Nothing. . . . It had merely occurred to me that this body which was touching mine would one day die and become carrion. For the first time, while performing an act which is the very symbol of life, I became aware of death."

"I experienced such a thing myself, two days ago," said Count Adam. "But what did your mistress think of it?"

"She must have conceived some rancour as a result, for the next day she came and threw stones against my bedroom window. . . . Ah! My dear Count, I know nothing more tragic than that despair of my twentieth year, when at an age to which all illusions are still permitted my own had already ceased to exist. . . . Had they ever existed? I possessed every advantage men covet and envy, and they were of no benefit to me. At the very moment I conceived some wish, my familiar demon whispered to me that it was a new illusion of which I would no more be the dupe than I had been of the others. I proceeded thus through the world, anxious, dissatisfied, my mind obsessed by that notion of death which blighted anything to which I tried to attach myself. It was as impossible for me to enjoy any pleasure which I knew would not be eternal, as it was to love a creature whom the least imperfection obliged me to abandon even before death could separate us, for I must admit that if I was obsessed by the idea of Oblivion, I was no less haunted by the notion of Perfection. By this word, I do not mean to designate beauty, of which it is difficult to give a precise description, but that kind of masterpiece constituted by any object or any being whose terrestrial cycle is completed forever. This led me to prefer old age to youth, the fall of empires to their inception, ruin and decadence to invention and energy. It is for this reason that I long sought out the society of old men. Of their almost completed lives, only a tiny portion escaped me—a few years, perhaps a few months. There lacked in the edifice of their existence, once I had patiently reconstructed it by my questions and my researches, only the consecration of an imminent end. My impatience for this event was occasionally so powerful that I was seized by the desire to kill. . . ."

"Did you ever commit such a crime?" asked Count Adam, horrified by this admission.

"No, but Heaven often did so in my place, and sometimes in so strange a fashion that I myself have actually felt remorse for it. I consequently assembled a number of documents intended to help me write the lives of persons whose obscurity was justified by their unimportance, but I wearied of this labour at the same time that I grew tired of Italy, of a sky so blue it seemed empty, of a sea as sparkling and hard as a sheet of polished steel. I regretted the melancholy of my childhood, vague and elusive as a dream upon waking, and I wished to recapture it once more. There is an infinitely soothing charm in the landscapes of the North. To see the waters of streams flowing sluggishly, to contemplate a sky where the play of clouds perpetually modifies a phantasmagorical universe—what indulgence for all the latent sadness I bore within me! I spent some time on our estate in Bohemia, until my father, who wished to see me follow his example, requested the Emperor to grant me a post in one of his embassies. I was sent to London. Do you know that city?"

"No," replied Count Adam. "I have never been there."

"London—this was in the days of the Regency—was an extremely gay city whose animation attracted me, but to which I soon came to prefer the surrounding countryside, where I made unforgettable sojourns in strange residences. England is the country of melancholy; the English language expresses all its nuances to a marvellous degree. I read poets who had made it the favorite theme of their works; I knew eminent men overwhelmed by this incurable disease. In some, it had reached the point of madness; in others, it remained a secret wound, dissimulated behind a façade of measured elegance, a rather bored arrogance. We spent entire days analysing our feelings, comparing their every nuance. When one of us, in order to translate a particular mood or explain a sensation so diffuse it was scarcely perceptible, hit upon a happy formulation, I experienced a sudden thrill of satisfaction, coupled with a certain bitterness, for I desired to advance as far in the quest of suffering as others in that of pleasure. This exploration of myself lasted for years, but it would not have been complete if I had not one day undergone a singular experience. In truth, I dare not give the name of experience to that sentiment which unexpectedly seized me, one afternoon, in Kew Gardens. . . ."

"What was it happened to you?" asked Count Adam, passionately interested.

"Nothing happened to me, once again. All my life, I have suffered only interior events. I was walking, then, in Kew Gardens when suddenly I felt myself become as light, as free as one of those globes of hot air released into the sky on holidays. Miraculously delivered of that burden which, for over twenty years, had made me the most miserable of men, I felt as though I was born anew into a marvellous world whose existence I had always divined without ever discovering it. Had I been favoured by a celestial apparition, I should not have known a greater ecstasy. I saw the landscape bathed in a supernatural light; the faces of passers-by were smiling; the water, the flowers, the very grass gleamed with an unwonted lustre. I felt I understood the murmurs of the breeze in the trees and the barking of the young mastiff that accompanied me. From deep within my being welled up the desire to associate myself more intimately with this universal joy. I longed to embrace a human body in order to communicate to it this ardour that was arousing my own. Intoxicated by an unknown happiness, I continued walking, and then, as suddenly as it had come, this dizzying sensation abandoned me. The sky suddenly darkened, the flowers lost their brilliance, the human beings their smiles. I found myself once again as anguished as I had been a few moments before, and for having enjoyed it for a brief moment I felt all the more sharply the privation of this felicity I so desired.

"I then embarked upon a second period of melancholy. Crueller, more intense than the first, it left me still less repose. I was haunted by images of death and corruption until I felt I was wasting away at each moment. The world was only a fragile vision which I constantly feared to see vanish before me.

Living each day as if it were to be my last, I had no other concern than to try to disengage from it an element which might
be eternal. Exhausting and lunatic task! My fondness for letters led me to presume that I was endowed in this realm. Alas!
Ideas thronged my mind without my being able to find the
words that would imprison them. The same was true for the
other arts I cultivated. My drawings were merely clumsy shadows; my paintings lacked that life I was so desperately seeking.
Only music helped me to translate my aspirations, but not my
own, and I blushed to borrow from others their personal
means of expression. Conceive of my desolation when I realized my absolute incapacity to create a work that would survive me! It was terrible. I nevertheless consoled myself for it,
knowing that no work would escape ultimate Oblivion and
that even renown that would endure until the end of time was
as ephemeral in the eyes of eternity as the glory of a day. I
thought of burying myself in some monastery to savour even
now the oblivion that was in store for me, but reached an altogether different decision: I married. My bride was the most
ravishing creature of all the United Kingdom, and I fell so
deeply in love with her that I supposed myself cured of that
melancholy which her presence so readily dissipated. Imagine
a young girl of slender figure, whose face was lit by enormous
green eyes fringed with black lashes . . . her complexion of a
freshness . . ."

As he spoke these last words, the old man began to tremble
in all his limbs, and his face turned ashen. His eyes widened
and fastened, horrified, upon a door behind the Count. The
latter turned around and remained transfixed with astonishment. In the frame of this door stood a young girl whose face,
a perfect oval, was illuminated by eyes the colour of emerald
accentuated by long black lashes. The dark mass of her hair
set off the dazzling whiteness of her complexion, the lustre of
her finely arched lips. Her aquiline nose, the harmonious line
of her brows, the noble curve of her forehead suggested the

perfection of Palladian architecture. Draped in an enormous shawl whose folds accentuated the majesty of her posture, she stood looking at the two men and smiling. She took a few steps towards them and spoke in German, but with a strong foreign accent:

"I beg you to excuse me, gentlemen, if I interrupt your conversation, but could one of you tell me if there might be found in the vicinity an inn more suitable than this one? My chambermaid and I arrived here about two hours ago, and we are already half devoured by the vermin that infest our bedchamber. . . ."

Count Adam turned back towards his companion. The latter had not stirred. His eyes remained fixed upon the door through which the newcomer had entered. His hands resting on the table, he had collapsed against the back of his chair in the attitude of someone felled by an unexpected blow. Although his mouth was open, no sound escaped from it. Alarmed, Count Adam leaned towards him and began to shake him: the body slipped from the chair and fell upon the floor with a soft noise. Upon hearing the cries of the Count and the newcomer, the innkeeper's wife appeared, followed by her son. The latter, with the Count's assistance, carried the inert body to a bed, but none of their efforts to revive him met with success. Death had come like a thunderstroke.

When the lovely stranger realized that her sudden appearance in the room had been its cause, she cursed Heaven for having been made the instrument of Destiny.

"Alas," she exclaimed, hiding her face in her hands, "why must it be that wherever I set foot I bring with me nothing but grief and desolation? After having seen all those I loved perish, must it now be that the mere sight of me is enough to cause even those I do not know to die?"

She sat upon a low stool, let her shawl slip from her shoulders and wept in silence for several minutes. Affected by such

42

distress but won by such charms, Count Adam remained standing beside her, and with great difficulty resisted the desire to take her in his arms the better to console her. The memory of Mademoiselle de Wabern returned quite opportunely to his mind and permitted him to find tears to mingle with those of the young woman. She appeared touched by this manifestation.

"I see, sir, that you are weeping for the loss of your friend. . . . Allow me to withdraw that you may be alone with him."

"Not at all, mademoiselle; I beg you, remain where you are! He was not my friend, I do not even know his name. We met here in this inn at the beginning of the evening, and we dined together by chance."

She raised her astonished eyes to meet his own.

"In that case, you must have a tender heart indeed to be so affected by the death of a stranger."

"Alas, mademoiselle, it is not for him that I am weeping, but for another, one who was dearer to me than all the world and who expired in my arms two days ago."

The young woman dried her tears and inquired with interest:

"Are you a widower?"

"No, mademoiselle, but I have had the immense grief of losing my fiancée, Mademoiselle Adélaïde de Wabern, and I am all the more overcome in that I despair of being able to marry at all. I had already been betrothed twice before and both my first fiancées died as well."

The lovely stranger seemed particularly interested by this revelation.

"What a strange coincidence! Imagine, sir, that I too have three times been betrothed, and that a cruel fate has robbed me of each of my three suitors."

Both young people agreed that the convergence of two histories so bizarre and so tragic was indeed a matter of great curiosity, and Count Adam urged the young woman to tell him the circumstances of her bereavements.

"To do that," she replied, "I must first speak briefly of myself and of my family."

She gathered up her shawl and wrapped it about her with a shiver, then began her tale.

"My name is Eva Scott-Birdson and I was born," she said, wiping away a tear that gleamed on her eyelid, "with the gayest disposition that can be imagined. The misfortunes with which the course of my existence has been strewn have not altered this happy nature. I may weep tonight, evoking such painful memories, but tomorrow I shall again be a heedless, flirtatious and frivolous young woman."

"I await the dawn with impatience," the Count murmured.

"I am British," she continued, without appearing to take note of this remark. "My mother too was English, daughter of the fifth Duke of Brightwalton, but my father belonged to one of the most considerable families of the Holy Roman Empire. Embarked in early youth upon a diplomatic career in which his own father had already distinguished himself, he was appointed to London and achieved in society the successes which his intelligence, his rank and particularly the charm of his person deserved. . . ."

"What was his name?" inquired the Count eagerly.

"Permit me, sir, not to disclose it. My mother made me take a vow never to pronounce it again, and I would not oppose the wishes of a dead woman . . . a woman, indeed, who died on his account! By marrying my mother he formed one of those unions which satisfy the desires of the families involved and complete the work of nature, for both young people were marvellously matched. My mother was one of the most delicious young women in London Society of the time, and her marriage disappointed many young men who sought her hand, though she had no fortune of her own. I have kept no recollection of my childhood years, and for this reason I know them to have been cloudless. The first catastrophe that fell upon our house was the disappearance of my father. Every morning, my governess brought me first to my mother's dressing room, where I would greet her, and then the two of us would visit my father, with whom I would spend about a quarter of an hour before luncheon. He would kiss me, ask me questions about my games, tease my dog and sometimes give me some small present. These brief moments were, for me, the best of the entire day. One morning, however, when we entered my father's study, we saw to our great astonishment that he was not there. My mother left me and went into his bedchamber. It was empty; the bed had not been occupied during the night. She supposed that he had gone to his club and been detained there so late into the night that he had preferred to stay for the remainder. She sent a footman to inquire, who returned with the intelligence that my father had not been seen. She waited the entire day, in the greatest distress, but my father did not appear, and the following day she informed the police, who searched the entire city and its environs. The Thames was dragged, but neither my father nor his body was found. The mystery remained unplumbed. This inexplicable disappearance caused a great scandal in Society, and despite my mother's prohibitions, the gazettes devoted a number of articles to the event. It was claimed that he had fled with another woman, that he had borrowed an immense sum of money and had vanished in order not to repay it. It was even said that he was an adventurer who had usurped an illustrious name in order to marry the daughter of a member of the English aristocracy. In short, the most extravagant rumours circulated, and were reported to us. My poor mother was so deeply affected that her health began to suffer. She was obliged to retire to the country. Her problematical position made her moods querulous and difficult. Passionately attached to her husband, she did not know whether she was to mourn him as dead or execrate him for having abandoned her. In my heart of hearts, I nourished the conviction that my father was not dead and that he would one day return. In an album which had been given me on the occasion of my birthday I began to write everything I could learn about him. In it I transcribed the recollections of his friends; I consigned to these pages my mother's stories as well. It was the only means I had of keeping my father alive in my memory, for I must tell you, sir, that my father's was a character singular enough to deserve a more exhaustive memorial than this collection inspired by filial piety: admirably gifted in all the arts, he could not decide to which to devote himself, and perpetually hesitated between literature or painting, music or drawing. He enjoyed all and attached himself to none. Far from turning his head, his successes afforded him, I was told, a kind of disenchantment which my mother vainly attempted to counteract. I suspect now that he was not happy and that he may have disappeared in order to attempt to find elsewhere, under some other sky, in some remote land, that happiness to which he aspired."

The young woman seemed a prey to an intense exaltation. She stood up and began to walk feverishly to and fro in the room. Her shadow lengthened or diminished as she left or returned to the candlestick that illuminated this scene. Count Adam wondered if he was not dreaming.

"Ah, sir! I am certain that my father is still alive and that he is in concealment somewhere. It is in order to find him that I have come to this country. I shall question everyone, I shall search the houses, I shall stop the very vagabonds on the roads, and I shall at last discover where he is hiding!"

Count Adam experienced a great joy at the thought that he was the master of this radiant creature's destiny and that with a word he could annihilate all her hopes. He nevertheless encouraged her to continue her narrative.

"I have told you that the various misfortunes which have characterized my youth did not exhaust the spring of happiness that flows within me, and I thank Heaven for this, for it is in no small measure that trials have come upon me. My father's disappearance deprived my mother and myself of the greater share of our fortune. Indeed, the entail of Bohemia passed to a nephew of my father's, and my mother had no other resources than a pension from her uncle, the sixth Duke of Brightwalton. We lived in the simplest manner imaginable, and I should have been content with such mediocrity if my mother's health had not suffered the consequences. She longed for her life of Society, her friends in London, and could not console herself for her husband's disappearance. She died of despondency, entrusting me to one of her childhood friends, who completed my education. I grew up loving her daughters as sisters, and believed I felt the same fraternal sentiments for her son, when one day I realized that the bond which united us was a stronger one. His mother realized this in her turn and appeared to be less delighted, for she anticipated an advantageous marriage for him, and I was penniless. She had not the heart to send me away from her house, but sent her son to join one of his uncles, a merchant in the Indies. Alas! He died there of a tropical fever, and I never saw him again. . . . I was sixteen, and at this age there is no despair which can resist the ardour of youth. A year later, I met a handsome cavalier at a County Ball who turned my head completely. He was rich, well born, amiable, and my adoptive mother immediately considered him with a favourable eye. His suit was accepted and my benefactress decided to give a party on the occasion of my betrothal. The entire county was invited, and from the dawn of the great day the entire household was a prey to the liveliest agitation. The girls whom I called my sisters were waiting with almost as much impatience as I myself for the arrival of my handsome fiancé, and I can still see myself waiting with them, watching for his arrival from behind the window of my room. We saw the first carriages turn in the courtyard to deliver the guests at the door. Soon everyone had arrived, and only the one for whom all our hearts were beating was still absent. The hour of the banquet passed without his appearing. A man was sent on horseback along the road my betrothed was to take. Anxiety was beginning to seize us all; the tone of the conversations had sunk to a disconsolate whisper. I divined some misfortune. Early in the afternoon, the horseman returned, shortly followed by a carriage in which my fiancé was lying, his spine broken by a fall from his horse. He expired during the evening, imploring me to forget him and not to waste my life on his memory.

"Yet that was my intention, and when, three months later, I received a visit from one of his close friends who desired to have from my own lips the account of his last moments, I was reluctant to receive him. His insistence managed to persuade me. I saw him, and we wept together. Upon taking his leave, he asked my permission to write me from time to time in order to evoke the memory of our friend; deep in his eyes burned a tiny flame of gaiety that cheered me and restored my spirits. Dare I admit that I waited for his first letter with impatience? In the secluded life I was leading, mail was the chief distraction, and soon a regular correspondence was established between us. In the meantime, an old uncle of my mother's had died, bequeathing me his entire fortune on condition that I take his name. It was thus that I became Lady Eva Scott-Birdson and that I went to live in the manor house of Great Houghton, in Wales. One spring morning Lieutenant James Herwyn came to visit me there, and we engaged in a long conversation at the far end of the grounds. When he left; I was no longer the same: a new joy dwelt within me. The future once again seemed full of promise, and I set about hoping for a better lot than had been mine. My joy was of brief duration. One day, reading the gazettes, I discovered that Lieutenant James Herwyn had been killed during a duel in a remote corner of Hyde Park. I flew to London and learned the details of this dreadful event. How shall I describe my grief? I returned to great Houghton, resigned to life, for a woman has not the courage to put herself to death, and spent an entire year in the greatest solitude. During this retreat, the thought of my father haunted me until I resolved to attempt the impossible in order to find him again. Is he not the only being who is left to me? Accompanied by my faithful Lydia, I embarked at Dover and after having traversed France and visited Italy, I arrived in Austria, where an obscure premonition tells me I shall discover my father."

"Yours is a story that would seem incredible to me if my own were not its counterpart," said Count Adam. "An orphan in early years, the heir to an immense fortune, I have seen languish and die three young women whose hands I successively sought. Am I, unknown to myself, the victim of some ancestral curse? What crime have I committed that fate should thus pursue me? Whom dare I ask to share my unhappy lot?"

"And to whom could I entrust my own?" the young woman sighed.

At this moment, the single candle that illuminated the room flickered, then went out, spent. Lady Eva exclaimed in alarm.

"Have no fear!" the Count said. "I shall manage to find us a light."

He was about to leave the room, but as he groped his way towards the door his fingers strayed over a shawl that parted like the curtains of a theatre to reveal two bare arms whose contact awakened his ardour.

Their embrace lasted so long that it was no longer necessary to seek a candle: the dawn surprised them in the common-room of the inn. The young woman gently disengaged herself and hastily repaired the disorder of her *toilette*.

"Let our happiness not prevent us from thinking of that poor soul who died here last night," she said. "I shall go and pray beside him for a few moments, then I shall awaken my chambermaid and we shall leave."

Count Adam de Stimmlicher remained alone, musing.

49

Never had the ways of Providence seemed more impenetrable to him, but for once they were manifesting themselves in his favour, and his soul overflowed with good cheer. He wakened the coachmen, who were asleep upon the straw beside the horses, and ordered them to harness the horses at once. Soon the carriages were at the door. The beautiful English girl, in her travelling cloak, mounted the step to her own carriage, and Count Adam sat down beside her. The chambermaid, with a pile of luggage, followed in the berlin. It was decided that the two carriages would proceed in this order.

The innkeeper's wife blessed the travellers and wished them every prosperity. Count Adam had left her two hundred florins to have the stranger suitably interred, and she was already planning to bury him at the back of her kitchen garden in order to avoid this expense.

The sky was of an admirable limpidity and only a few trees struck down by the wind attested to the violence with which the tempest had blown the day before.

Count Adam and Lady Eva were making a thousand plans for the future when suddenly they heard a dreadful crackling noise and felt the carriage capsizing in mid-air. The wooden bridge upon which the team had just advanced had collapsed. Swollen by the storm, the torrent that flowed beneath had weakened the foundations and the frail structure had yielded beneath the vehicle's weight.

Horror-stricken, Count Adam's coachman and Lady Eva's chambermaid saw their master and mistress perish without being able to afford them any help whatsoever. In a few moments, the current had completely scattered the wreckage of the carriage, and when the last debris had been swept away, the faithful servitors took the road back to the inn, convinced that nothing could withstand the Force of Destiny.

The Devil at Stillbad

■■■ ONE JUNE AFTERNOON, in the year 1822, the calm of ■■■
a little spa known as Stillbad was suddenly disturbed by
dreadful cries emanating from the Hotel Kronprinz Wilhelm,
the best establishment of its kind in the locality. Supposing
that a murder was being committed there, some twenty courageous persons dashed off in various directions to obtain assistance. Windows and balconies were filled with alarmed
faces emerging from huge napkins, for it was dinnertime. The
cries continued to grow louder and more terrible, and soon the
door of the inn flew open before a boy, some ten years old, pursued by a lady of majestic carriage. She was dressed in an extremely elegant mauve gown with yellow flounces, and wore a
bonnet of the same colour embellished with white plumes. She
was holding a crop in her hand and attempted to restrain the
child, who shrieked as he struggled.

Murmurs rose from the depths of the crowd, and such
words as "monster" and "unnatural mother" were audible
from the mouths of the curious.

A young woman, whose fastidious style of dress indicated a
superior condition, clapped her hands and exclaimed: "A
gown by Leroy!" and fainted dead away. She was immediately
carried from the scene. The twenty courageous persons, having become fifty, attempted to rush upon the stranger in order
to wrench her unfortunate victim from her, but an imperious
gesture checked their impulse.

"Who would dare keep me from beating my son?" she demanded haughtily.

"Your son, madame?" inquired the Burgomaster, whom

municipal duty had pushed into the front row. "What has he done to incur your wrath? Why are you punishing him so cruelly?"

"Because he has red hair!" the lady replied, in a tone of defiance.

The Burgomaster decided he was dealing with a mad-woman and insisted no further, but the good people of Still-bad, offended by such cynicism, seemed about to offer violence to the woman. They surged forward once again towards the steps leading to the door. And once again a gesture on the la-dy's part brought them to a standstill.

"But who are you, madame?"

"I am the Princess Dollintzky von Dollnitzau zu Dollnit-zach und Dollnitzberg!" she answered quite simply.

At these words, the Burgomaster, for whom the reading of the *Almanach de Gotha* was an everyday occupation, bowed re-spectfully four times in a row.

"I am at the orders of Your Most Serene Highness, but I en-treat her to be good enough to return to the hotel, as I cannot answer for my fellow citizens."

At the same moment an old servant in livery appeared, ac-companied by a coachman similarly garbed. They seemed to have been soundly thrashed, and were rubbing their limbs with grimaces of pain.

"Ah! There you are at last, imbeciles! Where have you been?"

"May Madame the Princess kindly excuse us," they stam-mered together, "but we have been unable to move for several minutes, and we can scarcely walk . . . His Highness must have cast a spell on us in order to make his escape!"

"Enough of that," the Princess interrupted. "Back inside, all of you!"

"Might I be useful in some respect to Your Highness?" in-quired the Burgomaster, upon whom the beauty of the illus-trious personage had produced a powerful impression.

She glanced at him sharply, stared into his eyes and then added in a more amiable tone:

"I believe you can, monsieur; come with us, if you will. You may help these two men hold Franz down, while I finish correcting him. The innkeeper's people are boobies who refuse to render me this little service."

The Burgomaster trembled, but his desire to learn more about this strange woman and the attraction she exerted upon him determined him to follow her. The innkeeper, trembling in every limb, closed the door behind them and the townspeople of Stillbad reluctantly dispersed. Their Burgomaster's acquiescence in seconding the traveller's caprice indicated to them that she must indeed be a lofty personage, demented no doubt, but all-powerful. That very evening, all Stillbad was whispering that the mysterious stranger lodging at the Hotel Kronprinz Wilhelm was a sister of the Emperor Napoleon, and she was forthwith nicknamed "The Ogress". The inhabitants barricaded themselves inside their houses, for fear she might come and carry off their children in the course of the night. Their apprehensions appeared all the more well-founded when, during the half-hour that followed The Ogress's withdrawal into the hotel, they heard a succession of the most ear-piercing shrieks. Their alarm would have known no limits had they been able to witness the singular spectacle their Burgomaster observed and in which he even participated.

After having returned to the apartment she occupied in the hotel, the Princess had asked the three men to hold the child firmly, and, armed with her crop, she had begun beating the young Prince with all her strength. The latter, screaming like a soul in Hell, struggled so vigorously that on three separate occasions he escaped, and occasioned the greatest difficulties in effecting his recapture. He ran about the room with an agility that bordered on the marvellous. To his stupefaction, the Burgomaster had even seen the child scale the bed curtains and take refuge upon the baldaquin, whence it had been no easy matter to dislodge him. But this was not his only occasion for astonishment, for the manner in which this apparently frail child endured the Princess's blows was quite properly incredible. Only the faintest reddening appeared when the crop lashed across the skin of his head, his neck or his legs. His cries alone bore witness to his sufferings, though even these gave the impression of cries of rage rather than of pain. The Princess wielded her crop with an energy which impelled admiration and inspired terror. She struck unremittingly, with application and diligence; any target suited her: head, arms, legs, chest, back. Finally the wretched child showed signs of weakening and collapsed in his torturers' hands. His mother had then laid down her crop and collapsed in an armchair, requesting her bottle of salts. The Burgomaster hastened to let her breathe from it, while the two servants carried away their young master's inert body.

"How weary I am. . . ." she sighed, fanning herself. "I trust that dinner will restore me. Will you do me the pleasure, monsieur, of sharing my repast?"

"I trust Your Highness will excuse me," replied the Burgomaster in a sarcastic tone, "but I must go home and beat my children. . . ."

"Ah, monsieur, it is not at all gallant to mock a poor woman whose secret you have involuntarily surprised, and who is not so guilty as you imagine her to be. . . ."

"The respect I bear towards Your Highness forbids me to ask her questions she would doubtless consider too bold, but such extraordinary behaviour cannot fail to occasion surprise."

"I conceive your astonishment, and should like to satisfy a curiosity which is only natural, but you have happened, alas, upon a family secret which I have not the right to divulge. You may know only that I do not behave in this fashion out of cruelty, but from duty. It is now four years that I have been executing every day, at the same hour, this odious charge. What woman could endure such an ordeal? It has shaken my nerves to the marrow, and it is to restore them that I have come to take the waters at Stillbad."

"But why does Your Highness not appoint some domestic to perform this unhappy task?"

The Princess's face assumed a scandalized expression:

"What! Have my son beaten by lackeys? I could not think of such a thing! No one must lay a cane or even a hand upon a Dollnitzky, unless it be someone of the same blood. Indeed, it is for this reason that I alone, and the members of the Imperial Family, have the right to beat this child. The chief pleasure of my annual sojourn in Vienna is the possibility of having Franz corrected by one or the other of the young Archdukes. Archduke Ludwig, for example, who is half mad and spends all his time thrashing his orderly officer, is enchanted to render me this service!"

There was a knock at the door. It was a servant of the hotel who was bringing in the Princess's dinner. She made a gesture to indicate the table on which he was to leave her tray, but the poor waiter, panic-stricken by the cries he had heard, mistook the significance of this gesture and supposed that the Princess was about to beat him in his turn: he dropped the tray and took to his heels. The service was happily assured by the old footman and the coachman, the latter transformed into a *maître d'hôtel*.

The evening was spent in a most agreeable fashion. The Princess was not only beautiful, but cultivated, witty and amiable. The Burgomaster, at first intimidated at finding himself seated opposite a person of such high lineage, was soon put at his ease by the noble stranger's gracious manners. She wittily recounted several anecdotes concerning her travels and her latest stay in Vienna, then questioned her interlocutor with an expression of genuine interest which enchanted the latter. In his turn, he described the peaceful existence he was leading in Stillbad with his mother and sister, the simple pleasures he enjoyed in the company of his friends or in that of the invalids who flocked to the spa to take the waters during the fine weather, but even as he furnished this description he suddenly realized that such a life was not so agreeable as he claimed. Never had he known a happiness comparable to the one he was experiencing at this moment, and it saddened him to think that this evening would have no sequel. As though she had read his mind, the Princess said to him:

"Why should you not return to dine with me from time to time? Despite my rank and my innumerable connections, I am quite alone and consequently sensible of the evidences of friendship people are kind enough to tender me. Yours would be quite agreeable, and I hope you will consent to favour me. . . ."

The Burgomaster, flattered, murmured a phrase of thanks and asked permission to withdraw. The Princess Dollnitzky stood up. Her shawl slipped down, revealing admirable shoulders, white, firm and round, whose sight troubled the Burgomaster so greatly that he forgot the farewell compliment he had prepared. He kissed in silence the hand extended to him and was preparing to cross the threshold of the room, when a sudden thought flashed through his mind:

"If I return occasionally to dine with Your Highness, as she has been kind enough to invite me to do, must I also assist her . . . to . . . beat . . . as I did today?"

"Oh, monsieur, I would not inflict this ordeal upon you if your conscience is opposed to it. In general, my old servants, who are utterly devoted to me, suffice for the task; but tonight, for what reason I do not know, the change in climate perhaps, or the exasperation of the journey, Franz was more difficult than usual, and they were unable to remain the masters. Fortunately I caught him at the very moment he was running away, after having escaped from their hands. . . ."

"Will Your Highness permit me to ask her one last question?"

She did so with good grace.

"How does it happen that the young Prince manages to resist such treatment, which would kill any other child of his age? There is something truly diabolical about it. . . ."

At these words the Princess's countenance altered.

"Ah, monsieur, you know not how truly you speak: I have Satan for a son! Adieu, monsieur!"

And she closed the door behind him violently.

The Burgomaster restrained his desire to rush down the stairs four at a time in order to flee the Devil's spells as fast as possible. With dignity he crossed the great hall, where several notables of Stillbad were drinking their beer and discussing the scene of which they had been the witnesses. Some attempted to stop and question him concerning his interview with the Princess, but he decided it was futile to reveal to these people the precious news he had just learned. The first to be informed must be the Sovereign, who in recompense would perhaps bestow upon him the post of Chamberlain to which he had aspired for so many years.

"His Majesty's service!" he cried, to escape those who attempted to detain him. He ran all the way to his house, where his mother and sister, already informed of the recent events, were awaiting him with anxiety. He reassured them, and ordered the carriage to be made ready at once. The Sovereign was, in fact, at his summer residence of Lustighausen, about three leagues' distance from Stillbad, and, despite the lateness of the hour, the Burgomaster resolved to journey there immediately.

It was close to midnight when he arrived. He wakened the sentry, who almost fired on him, had himself announced to the Grand Marshal of the Court, who appeared in his nightshirt with the Order of the White Eagle across his trembling chest. He was extremely vexed to be disturbed in the middle of his night's sleep.

"Why all this uproar, Monsieur the Burgomaster? Is the town of Stillbad in flames? What brings you here at this hour?"

"Matters so grave that His Majesty must be informed of

them at once. Be so good as to tell him as much, I entreat you, Excellency!"

The Grand Marshal yielded to the Burgomaster's insistence, and informed him, some quarter of an hour later, that the King would grant him an audience in his bedchamber. Karl-Friedrich XXVII was celebrated for the austerity of his habits, as he had had, for over twenty years, the same mistress, a former nun whom the French Revolution had driven from her convent. The Burgomaster had forgotten the existence of this person, and he was extremely embarrassed upon finding himself before the Royal Couch. The Monarch and his mistress shared this emotion, but since both of them were wearing nightcaps that concealed at least three-quarters of their faces and were huddled in sumptuous lace shifts, they resembled each other so closely that the wretched Burgomaster, perplexed, inquired:

"Which of you is His Majesty?"

The nightcaps agitated their ribbons and emitted a series of grumbles that discountenanced him.

"May Your Majesty deign to forgive me, but I must speak to him in secret. It concerns the fate of the Crown itself!"

"You may speak before my dear Minette, insolent fool!" said one of the bonnets. "There is no secret that I do not share with her."

"Very well, Sire! You must know that the Devil is at Stillbad!"

This revelation produced an astonishing effect upon the former nun, who leaped from the bed and began to execute all manner of capers, uttering bizarre cries the while which the Burgomaster found obscene. Karl-Friedrich XXVII had risen in his turn, and attempted to calm his dear Minette, who would hear of no such thing. She pushed him away, called him "Fouqier-Tinville" and through her tears swore he would not violate her a second time. Summoned by all this noise, the Grand Marshal proposed going to fetch the Court Physician.

"No, just bring some Holy Water, the best year—that of the Pope's coronation!" the King commanded.

The Grand Marshal hastened away and returned with a phial whose contents he flung at the dear Minette's head. Her convulsions ceased as though by magic and she recovered her spirits. In order not to expose her to their loss once again, the Grand Marshal led her into an adjoining room, while the Burgomaster gave the King an account of the events he had witnessed. The old Sovereign appeared deeply impressed.

"I have seen many curious things in my life, but none has seemed as strange to me as this one. I know the Dollnitzky Princes: they are powerful lords, related to the Imperial Family, and by virtue of this cousinage we must treat the Princess with solicitude. I knew, too, that there existed a mystery in their House, of recent origin moreover, but I was unaware that there was witchcraft as well, for what you have seen is certainly witchcraft! I shall effect some researches in my archives, and you, for your part, will attempt to learn something from the Princess's own mouth."

"Does Your Majesty not fear that her presence and that of her son might be a cause of disturbance in his domain? If the same scene recurs every day, it is to be feared that the inhabitants of Stillbad will not tolerate such a scandal, and in their indignation may be carried away to some regrettable extremity. . . ."

"That is true! Would it not be wiser to offer the Princess a residence somewhat sequestered from the town, where she may beat her son at her own discretion? Offer her, in my behalf, the Château of Traurighausen, which has been empty since my brother's death, and tell her that I will make it my duty to come and visit her there, once she is installed. Go now, Monsieur the Burgomaster, and if, as a result of your perspicacity, the Princess's sojourn passes without incident, I shall know how to remember the fact. . . ."

Upon this veiled promise, the Sovereign retied the strings of his nightcap and climbed back into bed. The Burgomaster left the room without turning around, his heart brimming with joy, and covered the road to Stillbad at a fast trot. He slept only a few hours, rushed the next morning to the Château of Trau-righausen to announce the Princess's arrival and to make certain that the most splendid apartments were prepared for her, recruited from the neighbouring châteaux a sufficient number of domestics for her service, and returned as rapidly to the town in order to pay her a visit before she had left the hotel. Upon crossing the Promenade des Etrangers, he passed two employees of the thermal establishment carrying a faint creature upon a litter. The Burgomaster recognized her as the young woman who had swooned the day before upon the Princess's appearance!

"A hat from Mademoiselle Normand!" he heard her murmur ecstatically.

"Heavens!" he realized at once. "The Princess is already abroad!"

He hastened on, and there at the turn of the path, among the other strollers but distinguishing herself from them by an almost ethereal gait, an inimitable grace and a truly superb carriage, he saw her. She was dressed in a puce riding-habit of an exquisite sobriety, and upon her head wore a ravishing bottle-green hat embellished with white plumes that trembled with the least breath of wind, the least movement. She seemed to hover in the balmy air this morning, and her son, who accompanied her, had the candid, smiling face of the *amoretti* that one sees fluttering about the goddesses in allegorical paintings. Charmed by this delicious scene, the Burgomaster stopped a few paces away and described a series of learned figures with his hat, then made a kind of obeisance one might have taken for a step from the *gigue*, and finally came to rest on one knee at the Princess's feet. He protested in florid language his sentiments of admiration and his respectful devotion to Her Highness. The child gave him a thousand caresses while the mother raised him to his feet with a few kind words. He asked her permission to escort her to the spring, and while she was drinking the salubrious waters in delicate sips, he transmitted to her his Sovereign's invitation. She appeared to be delighted by the favour.

"If I had not been obliged to leave in so hasty a fashion, I would have attempted to rent some estate in the environs, and I intended in fact to employ my afternoon finding a suitable lodging, for it is scarcely possible for me to sojourn long at the Kronprinz Wilhelm, where our presence is a cause of alarm as much for the innkeeper as for the other travellers, who are deserting the premises one after the other."

A silence fell.

"Wretched creature," the Burgomaster was thinking, "what malediction so burdens you?"

"The consideration you lavish upon me and the sincere interest you seem to show in my behalf make it my duty to apprise you of the truth of the strange situation in which I find myself. Who knows? Perhaps you can help me. . . . But this place is hardly propitious to confidences, and we shall wait until we are alone this evening to discuss the matter."

"I suspected, madame, that Your Highness's conduct, however bizarre it may have seemed, was certainly dictated by grave motives whose secret I am bound to respect, and I do not wish, for the price of whatever slight services I may hope to render Your Highness, to induce her to betray this secret."

"Ah, monsieur, do you not suppose that it is sometimes sweet to open one's heart to that of an honest man, and to find in his confidence a balm for one's own torments?"

"Affecting creature! Unfortunate and affecting creature!" the Burgomaster mused with growing emotion, while his companion raised to meet his own a pair of superb black eyes in which he saw the tears welling. He took her hand and bore it to his lips with an infinite respect. She showed no offence at this audacity, and gave him a rendezvous after lunch to take her to Traurighausen.

As they were returning, the sun began to decline.

"Great God!" she exclaimed. "I must reach the hotel at once! It is time to beat Franz."

The Burgomaster dared not leave her. They found Prince Franz drawing by himself, in the most peaceful manner in the world. He greeted his mother's return with manifestations of joy which the Burgomaster considered surprising. A few minutes later, the old servant and the coachman slipped silently into the room and bolted the doors. Six-thirty sounded. The child suddenly turned livid, his red hair gleamed like so many tiny flames, and he began to utter raucous cries that resembled the howls of a wild beast. Immediately the two servants rushed upon him and struggled to master him. His mother, beautiful as an offended Juno, seized the crop and began to beat him. Twice the young Prince escaped, and the Burgomaster, who was the most agile of the three, was obliged to climb onto a table in order to dislodge him from the chandelier, to which he clung, despite his weight. This prodigy, joined to that of being able to rise into the air, struck the Burgomaster with a stupor, and he was quite relieved when at seven the child's convulsions ceased. He gradually calmed down, recovered his habitual colour, and the traces of the blows he bore on his face, neck and hands finally disappeared altogether. He politely wished the Burgomaster a good night, kissed his mother's hand, and left the room.

"Madame, this child is possessed!" exclaimed the Burgomaster, who had some inkling of such matters, having one day attended the exorcism of a farmer's daughter.

"Alas, monsieur, you are right, but no human or divine power can drive out the Evil Spirit when it seizes him. The Archbishop of Bud himself has attempted to do so, without success. He gained only a terrible rain of blows, applied by an Invisible Hand, and as a result of this experience was obliged to take to his bed for over a month. It is, in fact, a curse that hangs over our House; one which, I fear, will only disappear when it does. My son is the last Prince Dollnitzky, and I hope that with him the name will be extinguished, but the designs of Heaven and those of Hell are impenetrable. It is futile to attempt to modify them. . . ."

She sighed deeply several times over. Dinner was served, and they sat down to table.

"The account I am about to give you, my dear friend, is not at all the fruit of my imagination, as its improbability might lead you to believe. It is based on certain traditions, certain legends of the country, but also on the memoirs of the first Prince Dollnitzky, completed by the notes of his descendants and the letters I have discovered while searching through the archives at Dollnitzschloss. Upon my widowhood, I spent two years there, and during this retreat I had leisure to reconstitute this sad story in its entirety. . .

"It begins with that of the Dollnitzkys: the first Prince Dollnitzky was in reality called Peter Zurcher. Despite his mother's youthful liaison with Count Dollnitzky, the child had not a single drop of this illustrious seigneur's blood in his veins, though it pleased him to believe that he did. He was quite legitimately the issue of one Karl Zurcher, a groom in the Count's service, and of Mathilde, a former chambermaid of the Countess's. Both lived in modest lodgings near the stables, and it was there that Peter grew up, amid the braying of horses and his father's oaths, the kicks of the former and the blows of the latter. At the age of ten years he was presented at the château and joined to the numerous domestics who were tyrannized by a major-domo. His role was of minor importance indeed: each morning, he accompanied the Countess to Divine Service in order to carry her missal. He spent the rest of the day in one of those huge, glacial antechambers where the valetry awaits orders. Was it during those long hours of ennui that his young and eager imagination let itself be swept away by wild dreams, and that he dreamed of one day becoming his masters' equal? No one will ever know, for even in his private memoirs he never dwells upon this period of his existence, but it is certain that, early in life, he manifested the desire to raise himself above his condition. This pretention was received unfavourably by the very beings who might have rejoiced over it. His father gave him a vigorous correction; his mother, alarmed, made him a thousand reproaches. Both found themselves opposed by a fierce determination which they did not succeed in shaking. The child, some time afterwards, informed the Countess that his parents were mistreating him, and obtained permission to live henceforth under the roof of the château, with the other servants of the house. He was intelligent, lively and servile. He rapidly won the Countess's favour, and when he reached the age of eighteen she gave him to the Count in order to have an ally near her husband, of whom she lived in terror. Peter lost no time in winning the latter's confidence as well, and grew accustomed to betray each of his masters to the other's advantage and invariably to his own as well. This brilliant result, which excited the jealousy of the other domestics, was nevertheless a small thing in comparison with his aspirations, but he did not yet see by what means he would realize them, when chance made his decision for him.

"One evening the Count summoned Peter in order to inform him that for several days he would be attached to the person of one of his guests, a stranger who would be travelling without a valet. Peter immediately conceived a great contempt for a personage of such unimportance, and was astonished that his master should deal with him at all. The anticipated guest arrived three days later with a modest luggage which Peter carried into the bedchamber reserved for him. The stranger's appearance was nondescript. He was dressed in black from head to foot, without the least ornament, and spoke little. Nonetheless, when Peter had finished putting away his effects, the stranger turned to him and in a weary voice remarked:

" 'Why is there such bitterness in your heart? Take courage! One day you shall be a greater lord than your master. . . .'

"Peter dropped the torch he was holding. He bent to pick it

up again and, his face pale as death, fixed the stranger with his eyes.

" 'Who are you, then, to divine the secrets of other men in this fashion?'

"The stranger smiled.

" 'My name, or rather the name under which I am known upon my travels, will teach you nothing. You may know only that I am more powerful than the Count, since he has need of me, and that I can read men's hearts. Therefore do not despise me because I have neither valet nor carriage, and do not fear me because I tell you these things. That would embarrass you in asking me to do you a service, although you have few scruples, is it not so?'

"Peter, terrified, stared at the face that bent towards his own with a smile, the eyes gleaming with an almost unendurable brilliance.

" 'You are the Devil!' he murmured, and attempted to flee, but a force superior to his own will kept him from doing so.

" 'No, I am not the Devil,' sighed the stranger, with an air of regret. 'I am only a man. . . . Does the Devil really exist?'

"He took up a book, some paper, opened a travelling ink-well, and, suddenly turning away from his interlocutor, began to write. Then Peter left the room and descended to the pantries in order to glean there some information as to the mysterious guest. The noisy atmosphere below stairs restored his assurance, but he learned nothing that might inform him further as to the stranger. The coachman who had been sent to meet him at the nearest post inn did not even know his name. All the servants agreed in declaring that he was a man to avoid, and no one could explain on what caprice the Count might have invited him to Dollnitzschloss. The following days passed without his leaving his room, where he abandoned himself to the most curious occupations. Several alchemical instruments had been installed there, notably an alembic, and each morning the Count spent long hours with his guest. Peter served his meals, cleaned the room, brushed his clothes, but, although devoured by curiosity, dared not address a word to the man. One evening, however, as he was about to withdraw, he heard his name called out:

" 'Peter, you would like to know if what I predicted for you the other day will prove to be true, wouldn't you? I shall give you the details that you are longing to know. Sit down and show me your hand.'

"Peter obeyed and held out his right palm.

" 'I read hands even better than hearts. . . . You shall be, as I have told you, a greater lord than your master, and you shall realize all your desires, but take care: you will attain all your desires only in exchange for your own soul!'

" 'Must I sell my soul to the Devil?' murmured Peter, who at this moment recovered the fervent piety of his childhood, for it seemed to him that Hell itself was opening before him.

" 'You will never sell anything to anyone,' the alchemist replied. 'Hear me out, I shall reveal a deep secret to you. I shall die soon, for the last time I hope, and I know not to whom to confide it. I would not give it to your master: he is a covetous man who supposes—quite wrongly, moreover—that I can create gold. It is for this reason that he has invited me here. I know not the secret of gold, but that which I am about to tell you is a far more precious one. If men were to know it, perhaps they would be more prudent. Listen well, Peter: Heaven and Hell do not exist. God and the Devil, on the other hand, exist indeed, and it would be a great sin to deny it. The souls of the dead do not rise up, therefore, to sing the glory of the Lord in Paradise or descend to burn in Hell for Eternity. The souls of the dead return to earth in a new body, in order to expiate their crimes, their follies, or to receive the rewards they deserve. It is for this reason that you see people who are inexplicably happy, for whom existence is a perpetual feast, whereas others are overwhelmed by an unjust fate. The great sinners who die unpunished are reincarnated in a different form and are condemned to lead as many wretched lives as they have accomplished misdeeds. Often it happens that they are their own descendants. This explains why dynasties perish, why empires collapse, why cities vanish. . . . Can one conceive a more terrible punishment? Why are men unwilling to be content with what is given them? Never forget this, Peter. Each time you ask something bad of fate, you must return to this world to expiate such foolish desires once they are granted.'

"He rummaged in his papers, took out a bundle of documents and selected one which he gave to Peter. It was a half-sheet of parchment, covered with tiny, close-set handwriting.

" 'Here, take this. It is not the formula of the transmutation of metals, but merely a discovery which I made long ago and which I have not had the opportunity to exploit. It will make you a rich man, and you will have no need to force your luck nor to engage your soul.'

"Peter, somewhat disappointed, for he would have preferred a magic ring, some such talisman as a moonstone or a seal, nevertheless thanked the stranger effusively.

" 'Now leave me. I must prepare myself.'

"Peter withdrew. He was not entirely convinced by these strange remarks, and, reasonably enough, sought to convince himself that he had had dealings with a madman. Having returned to his own room, he attempted to read the paper. To his great chagrin, he discovered that it was written not in German but a language which seemed to him to be Latin. Had the alchemist been mocking his credulity and merely given him a worthless paper? Perplexed, Peter folded it carefully and put it in the hiding-place where he kept his money.

"The evening of the same day, at the moment he was about to knock at the alchemist's door, he heard from within the room the sound of a violent argument. The Count, whose voice he had recognized, appeared to be in the greatest rage, and rudely insulted his guest. The latter replied quite calmly.

" 'Dog!' shouted the Count. 'I want gold. You can make it,

and if you fail to do so, it is only because you will not obey me. . . .'

"Then his voice assumed a supplicating tone:

" 'I must have gold, you understand! I must have it. If I do not pay back the sums I have borrowed from the Treasury of the Chamber of Lords, the Emperor will be merciless. . . .'

" 'His Majesty is just! He chastises thieves, even when they are of a rank as high as that of Your Excellency. . . .'

"The Count uttered a roar of fury:

" 'You dare call me a thief, insolent! Ah!'

"There was a muffled thud, followed by the sound of something falling. Peter, beside himself, opened the door: the alchemist was lying on the floor, senseless. Blood was flowing from his head, out of a great wound. A log of firewood in his hand, the Count was staring at his victim in a stupor. His valet's entrance caused him to drop his weapon, which rolled to the stranger's feet.

" 'If you can hold your tongue,' he said quickly, 'I shall know how to reward you.'

"Peter, trembling in every limb, promised to keep the secret, and helped his master to wrap the corpse in a great cloak. They washed away the bloodstains.

" 'Tonight, when everyone is asleep, we shall bury him in a corner of the park, and no one will be able to say what has become of him.'

"No one, indeed, remarked on the stranger's disappearance, and at the château it was believed that he had departed as mysteriously as he had come.

"Now that he was in possession of three secrets, Peter could no longer sleep for brooding over them, and wondered which way to utilize them in order to begin making his fortune. The stranger's death had profoundly impressed him, less by its tragic character, moreover, than by the presentiment which this unfortunate person had had of it. 'I shall die soon, for the last time, I hope . . . ,' he had said. Peter had not questioned the stranger as to the meaning of this curious remark, but afterwards he had been struck by it. What mystery did it conceal? Had the stranger already lived other lives, and had he been obliged to return to earth in order to expiate some abominable action? The secret of the Count's financial embarrassments intrigued him also. Had his master actually embezzled large sums? Everything pointed to this conclusion, for every day the Count's brow grew increasingly careworn, and Peter knew him well enough to be certain that it was not remorse for his crime that was tormenting him to this degree. The year before, he had shot two peasants guilty of not having saluted him as he passed, and that had altered his fine humour not one whit."

The Princess broke off. Although the candles were guttering, the Burgomaster could see that she was extremely pale and appeared about to swoon. He offered to call a servant to bring her a cordial.

"No, dear friend, there is no need, but I shall not tell you more tonight, for I am at the limit of my strength. It has always been claimed that I was gifted with certain supernatural powers. This notion is exaggerated, and I am no sorceress, rest assured, but it is true that I can evoke facts, describe events that have occurred long before my birth. Often I have entered into communication with Peter's damned soul, and I have been able to question him concerning all that I did not know about his life. This requires, alas, an effort of the mind, a power of concentration which exhausts me. . . ."

She smiled wearily and gave her auditor leave to withdraw, fixing a rendezvous with him for the following day at the Château of Traurighausen, where, upon the Sovereign's invitation, she was to establish her residence.

The next evening the Burgomaster presented himself at the château. He had calculated that if he arrived at seven the young Prince's daily fit would have passed, and that he would thereby be spared the dreadful spectacle. Indeed, all was calm in the vicinity of Traurighausen, and only the croaking of the frogs broke the evening silence, perfumed by the odour of the lindens. The Princess was waiting for him, sitting on the terrace. She was dressed in a *négligé* which revealed her shoulders almost entirely, and the Burgomaster regretted the cowardice which he had evidenced by arriving so late for this intoxicating rendezvous. He sat at the noble lady's feet and seized the hand she abandoned to him. The twilight lent them its complicity.

"Ah, my friend," she murmured, "how sweet is the air, and what consolation your presence brings me in this solitude. . . ."

She mused a moment, then withdrew her hand.

"But I am forgetting that you have come to hear the end of my story. Will I have strength to complete it?" she added anxiously.

"I prefer, madame, the repose of Your Highness to the satisfaction of my curiosity, and I entreat her not to continue this story which must be so painful. . . ."

"No, I wish you to know the truth. . . . Where had I stopped in my narrative when we parted yesterday? Ah, yes, I had reached the proposition which young Peter made to his master. No doubt it is the sole trait of kindness which can be found in Peter Zurcher's entire existence: seeing the cares that overwhelmed the Count, he revealed to him that the alchemist had left him a secret capable of making his fortune. And was his chief duty not to help his benefactor to re-establish his own? At these words, the Count supposed that Peter possessed the secret of making gold, and his face lit up. It immediately darkened again upon learning that there was no question of creating gold, but he nonetheless appeared extremely curious as to this formula. Considering the desperate circumstances in which he found himself, ought he not to try everything? Peter brought him the paper which, in his turn, the Count vainly attempted to decipher. Fortunately, the Countess's Chaplain managed to do so without too much difficulty, and gave him the translation of the text, which was written in Italian. It was a new means of manufacturing porcelain paste. The Count determined to experiment with it on the spot.

"A few hours later, shut up in the very room where he had committed his crime and assisted by Peter, the Count was mixing, decanting, grinding and measuring according to the prescription of the recipe. When the paste they had prepared emerged from the oven, they discovered with amazement that it was transformed into a piece of porcelain of so extraordinary a fineness that it was translucid. Assuredly such a discovery was worth a fortune, and the stranger had not lied. In the weeks which followed, Peter and the Count busied themselves with other attempts, all of which were crowned with success. They even fashioned several small objects, of coarse form, indeed, but sufficient to show the delicacy of this miraculous porcelain. The Count had no time to lose. He left for Vienna in order to spread the news there and to find the support necessary for the creation of a manufactory. This discovery caused a great deal of talk, and in less than six months all the difficulties were surmounted. The Count readily persuaded the Emperor that the large sums he was accused of having embezzled had merely been borrowed from the Chamber of Lords in order to permit him to continue his researches, whose secret he wished to keep until their success. He received the Imperial pardon, and His Majesty, in order to encourage him to found the first manufactory, gave him a hundred thousand florins from his privy purse.

"Soon nothing was talked of, in Court and capital alike, save the new porcelain, whose inventor was in great demand. It was a cause of amazement that so noble a lord should possess so great a genius and condescend to employ it. The Count achieved such successes that he forgot the being to whom he owed them. He had also forgotten the existence of his wife. This latter, anxious over so long an absence, dispatched Peter to Vienna. He arrived there one fine morning, inquired as to his master's residence, and found him living in the greatest magnificence. The Count, at first, pretended not to recognize him, and then, when Peter demanded his legitimate share of this prosperity, laughed in his face.

"'What nonsense are you talking? You forget that you are my lackey, and that you possess nothing which does not belong to me!'

"Peter, outraged, attempted to protest, but the Count gave him no opportunity to do so, and had him thrown out the door at once. You can imagine the poor boy's despair, so unjustly cheated of what was his due. . . . His first thought was to reveal to the courts the murder his master had committed and thereby ruin him, but then he reflected that no one would credit the evidence of a mere domestic against a man so powerful as the Count. For several days he wandered through Vienna, seeking in vain the means to avenge himself. He constantly returned to the Count's palace and spent long moments staring at its façade. One morning, as he was standing before it, he saw the light barouche in which the Count visited the manufactory emerge from the canopy and turn into the square. The appearance of his enemy aroused the hatred he felt in his behalf.

"'Ah, scoundrel!' he said in an undertone, 'I wish that Heaven might punish you as you deserve!'

"No sooner had he spoken these words than an equipage of the Court debouched from a nearby street and passed so rapidly before the barouche that the latter's horses were startled. They took the bits in their teeth and set off upon a mad dash. The carriage caught on a kerb, overturned, and its occupant was projected upon the pavement. The passers-by rushed to his assistance, and Peter, who had preceded them, saw that the Count's head had knocked against a log, fallen no doubt from a cart delivering firewood. There was a great cleft in the brow, through which the blood flowed copiously. At this sight, Peter experienced a savage joy, mingled with fear. The Count had been killed in the same fashion that he had murdered his guest. Was this a coincidence or a chastisement? Was it, above all, the realization of the wish Peter had expressed a few seconds earlier? In this case, did he truly have the power to obtain what he desired in exchange for his soul? He could not believe it, and required another proof.

" 'I shall have it,' he determined, 'if I can recover possession of the formula that was stolen from me . . .'

"He was almost disappointed upon finding that the paper did not immediately appear in his hands. While he was planning a thousand schemes, the body of his former master was taken into the palace. Quite automatically, Peter followed the men who were bearing the corpse. Behind them, he entered the palace once again. Their arrival produced the greatest confusion. Taking advantage of this disorder, Peter wandered through the apartments at random, and finally found himself in the Count's study. He rummaged through the drawers of the desk, and then through those of a little secretary, and discovered a bundle of documents which he hastily examined: the parchment was there. He took possession of the entire bundle and fled. Having returned to the inn, Peter was able to give his plunder a closer examination. You can conceive his astonishment upon discovering that several letters were written in the same hand as that on the parchment. They were signed 'Cancellati' and the last of them announced the arrival of their author at Dollnitzschloss. The Count had been indiscreet enough to preserve them. Peter hastened to entrust all these documents to a poor girl with whom he had formed a liaison, and addressed a long letter to the Emperor. In it he recounted in detail the true story of the new porcelain, and asked that justice be done. The only difficulty was to cause this letter to reach the Emperor without its going astray in the pocket of some gentleman of the palace. The occasion presented itself in an unexpected manner. The gazettes announced that the Court would be represented at the funeral ceremonies of

Count Dollnitzky by Archduke Lamprecht. Peter took up his post along the route of the funeral cortège, and at the moment when the Archduke's carriage was before him he broke through the cordon of troops to hold out a petition. An *aide-de-camp* received it and handed it to the Prince, who inclined his head slightly.

"The week passed without further incident. Peter saw his poor resources rapidly diminishing, and he had resolved to leave the inn, where he could no longer pay for his keep, when one evening he was called for by order of the Minister of Justice. He was taken before this important personage and at his request retraced the strange events discussed in his letter. The proofs he was able to furnish, thanks to the documents abstracted from the Count's desk, managed to convince the Minister, who begged Peter not to bruit this matter about, and promised him that it would be settled in complete equity. For security's sake, Peter was held in secret for some time, and the best agent of the Imperial Police was sent to Dollnitzschloss. He received the Countess's confidences, interrogated the Chaplain, questioned the servants, and even exhumed Cancellati's corpse, which appeared in a wonderful state of preservation, as if it had just been deposited in the ground, and thus had no difficulty establishing the veracity of Peter's evidence. This latter was forthwith restored his legitimate property, and he took possession of the manufactory, whose development he had soon prodigiously extended by both industry and skill.

"In several years, he had made a considerable fortune. He purchased Dollnitzschloss from the ruined Countess and assumed the name. It was more difficult for him to obtain the concession of the title from the Emperor, but in the meantime the war against the Turks resumed and he equipped an entire regiment at his own expense. This patriotic gesture earned him the title of Prince of the Holy Roman Empire. Peter was then thirty-six or thirty-seven years of age. Far from taking pride in such a success, his parents were in despair over it:

when he had acquired the domain of his former masters, they left it to live in a sordid hovel. They told all who would listen that their son's fortune was accursed, and stubbornly refused to accept the least share of it. This arrogance excited the new Prince's wrath in the highest degree, for he no longer dared visit Dollnitzschloss for fear of being publicly insulted by his parents. His bailiff informed him of their every word and deed, and the day he learned that his father accused him of having made a pact with the Devil his fury knew no bounds. In the presence of a terrified servant, he broke the latest models of porcelain that had just been brought to him from the manufactory, shouting:

" 'May they perish in this wise, they and all my enemies!'

"In his next monthly report, the bailiff informed him that during an autumn tempest his parents had been killed by the collapse of the roof of their house. The rafters, which were rotten, had yielded under the violence of the wind.

"Did Peter recall the alchemist's prophecy? Did he under-stand that the realization of each of his wishes was precipitat-ing his fall? Intoxicated by success, he abandoned himself without apparent remorse to the joy of his triumph. His hap-piness would have been complete had he been able to share it with someone. He needed a wife, a Sovereign for Dollnitz-schloss, a slave for himself. He gave a series of balls at which the most ambitious of lovely women vied in intrigues for his hand. He ignored them, and his choice fell on the delicious Countess Karola von Mürtzingen, a creature so fragile and delicate that she seemed to have emerged from the Prince's own porcelain works. Unfortunately her father belonged to an illustrious House and refused to give his daughter to a former lackey, however rich and well-thought-of he might be. The Prince was in despair, grew furious, allowed his feelings to carry him away and resolved to be the master. He attempted to elope with the young Countess, but this experiment failed. Once again he had recourse to the dangerous power he possessed. He wished aloud that the young woman might become his own. A short time afterwards the Count von Mürtzingen lost a battle and was exiled to a distant land where he feared to die of ennui, for he was a frivolous and vainglorious man who loved only the life of the Court. The Prince's intervention procured his return to favour. The Countess Karola was the price of this negotiation. The marriage took place, but in the years which followed the poor lady brought into the world so many daughters that there were soon no longer enough Archduchesses to serve as their godmothers. Upon the birth of her ninth daughter, the Princess Dollnitzky perished. Her husband was greatly aggrieved, for he was still awaiting an heir capable of assuring the continuity of his dynasty. A second wife provided him one at last, but the Prince had meanwhile grown old; his health had altered and he fell so gravely ill that the physicians despaired of saving his life. He realized his condition, and was in great alarm over it. Now that he was approaching the end of his days, he recalled their beginning more frequently, even in the presence of his intimates, who had received orders never to allude to the obscurity of the Prince's origin. He recalled with anguish the prediction that had been made to him some forty years before. Would he be punished for the faults he had committed, for those desires that had been granted so strangely? For how many generations of his lineage would he be obliged to pay the debt he had contracted towards destiny? Was one of his children already bearing the burden of this malediction? Must his ambitious soul reincarnate itself as many times as he had wished for the impossible? The memory of the principal circumstances of his life, those in which he had forced chance itself, haunted him. In a kind of delirium which terrified his entourage, he recapitulated its course: the Count's accidental death, the manner in which he had recovered the formula for the porcelain, the death of his parents, his marriage. . . . This agitation was soon followed by such a prostration that the physicians judged his last hour had come and made way for his

Chaplain. When the latter approached the ceremonial bed upon which the Prince was lying in his last agony, an expression of terror was painted upon the dying man's visage. Could it be that death was already so close at hand? His bloodless lips emitted a few words which those persons standing nearest could hear:

"'My God! Let me live a little longer. . . .'

"He received the last sacraments, and the following day, to universal astonishment, he had somewhat recovered. A week later, he was walking, leaning on his secretary's arm; he visited the manufactory and resumed his habitual activities. It was at this period that he wrote his memoirs, but he was unable to complete them, for death surprised him before he had finished this task.

"The very evening of the day he expired, his son, aged ten years, was seized with strange convulsions which were attributed to the emotion caused by this event. After some time, it was decided that the child was the victim of a mysterious disease which no one could cure. It was the curse of the Dollnitzkys. At the end of every day, for half an hour, he fell into a kind of furious, almost bestial madness, and, if he was not watched closely, committed the most horrible acts. There was talk of epilepsy, of Saint Guy's dance, yet it was as impossible to discover the origin of this derangement as its remedy. The young Prince left Vienna and lived at Dollnitzschloss in the greatest isolation. When he attained his majority, he married a girl of great beauty but meagre fortune whom the fabulous wealth of the Dollnitzkys had seduced. She produced twin sons, then went mad and died in a convent. Her husband killed himself during a fit by throwing himself out of a window. At the moment he breathed his last, one of his sons uttered a series of shrill screams and began to execute a demoniacal dance beside his father's corpse. When he was subdued, he wept bitter tears. This spectacle produced so powerful an impression upon his brother that he lost the use of speech for almost a week. When he had recovered, he declared that he would ultimately retire to a monastery in order to expiate the crimes of his family. He is still alive, and is regarded as a saint. It was to his unfortunate twin brother that the duty of maintaining the Dollnitzky line fell. He married a Princess of the house of Les Trois-Ponts, linked to that of the Habsburgs. Her father, Duke Johann, had mistreated her to such a degree and rendered her life so odious that she preferred to become the wife of a Dollnitzky rather than remain under paternal authority. I must say that she fulfilled her role perfectly and did not let herself be alarmed by the Prince's disease. Her father had taught her the virtues of the crop. She wielded it masterfully upon her husband, who derived great benefit therefrom: the blows assisted him to combat the Demon's presence within himself. He was therefrom beaten every day by the Princess herself, but, alas, when she died no one was willing to replace her in the execution of this charge, and the Prince's existence, as well as that of his entourage, was considerably clouded. . . . This remarkable woman was my mother-in-law. . . ."

The Princess paused. The trees of the park rustled, and their branches appeared to stretch as far as the terrace. She shivered. Her companion immediately expressed some anxiety:

"The evening is cool. Does Your Highness not fear to take a chill?"

"You are right," she said. "Let us return indoors."

She accepted the Burgomaster's arm, and passed with him into the salon.

"You are certainly wondering what motive incited me to marry Prince Emmerich? It was not the attraction of his fortune, for my own permitted me to choose my husband quite freely. Alas, I was obliged, in order to save my reputation, to renounce the choice my heart had already made and consent to this union. On the side of his mother, the Princess of Les Trois-Ponts, we were cousins, and for this reason I was accustomed to make rather long stays at Dollnitzschloss. Members of the family were invited there in preference to strangers, who would certainly have surprised the dreadful secret and noised it about. For many years, my younger sister and I myself were the only companions of Prince Emmerich's boyhood. We knew what heredity burdened him, but great care was taken to conceal its manifestations from us. Moreover, the Princess had become accustomed to whip her son in a farmhouse near which the animals destined for the Schloss kitchens were slaughtered. Their cries drowned out those of my cousin. On the rare occasions when the Princess was prevented from doing so, her son, deceiving the surveillance of the domestics, committed, under the influence of the Demon that possessed him, many atrocious acts. Once he strangled a child in its cradle; another day, he kicked his favourite dog to death; and on a third occasion . . . I was, alas, his victim. . . . The Emperor and his train had come to hunt at Dollnitzschloss, and my future mother-in-law had not found the occasion to vanish at the habitual hour to join her son in the room where he was kept imprisoned. A few minutes before dinner, I was in my bedchamber, making a hasty toilet, for we had returned quite late from the hunt, when I heard a wild running in the hallway. Shoving aside my chambermaid, who attempted to prevent him from entering, Prince Emmerich, beside himself and uttering inarticulate cries, appeared. I wished to flee, but terror nailed me to the spot. He rushed upon me and had soon, despite my desperate resistance, reduced me to his mercy. My chambermaid had fainted and no one came to my rescue. Even before I had recovered my senses, the Prince, returning to his own, threw himself at my feet and implored me to marry him in order to make amends for this moment of madness. Bewildered, terrified, affected, too, by his sincere grief, I consented to do so. We walked together into the dining hall and announced our betrothal. The Emperor, delighted, immediately created me a Lady of the Palace, and everyone was content, particularly the Princess Dowager, who had given up hope of such a union for her son."

"Unfortunate creature!" groaned the honest Burgomaster. "I dare not think of the life which was yours thereafter!"

"Oh," she replied, "it was not so terrible as you suppose it to be. My husband did not make me unhappy. He was handsome, amiable, cultivated and witty, but I was forever anxious that he might kill me during one of his fits, and I nearly died of fear if I remained alone with him. He perished in a hunting accident, struck in the heart by a bullet intended for a poacher. My son, at this period, was six years old. The ancestral curse was transferred to him, and there is no day that passes when I do not fear some catastrophe. With him, however, the chastisement must come to an end, for he is incontestably the fourth incarnation of Peter Zurcher, and the latter, according to my calculations, formed only four wishes. The entire future of our house therefore rests upon his head, and I hope that his children will be delivered from this baneful enchantment."

"May Heaven hear Your Highness," the Burgomaster sighed fervently, "and may it accord this satisfaction for the oblivion of her torments."

"It seems to me that when I am with you, I already begin to forget them," the Princess replied, smiling with a divine expression.

Transported by these words, in which he found an undisguised encouragement, the Burgomaster leaned forward, and the Princess, abandoning her Most Serene Loftiness, fell into his arms.

Their *amours* lasted the entire summer and extended well into the autumn.

The Princess could not bring herself to leave the Château of Traurighausen. She had forgotten her cure, her friends and the diversions that awaited her in Vienna. One afternoon, while the lovers tarried in their felicity, she forgot her son as well.

That evening the Sovereign gave a last *fête* before leaving his summer residence of Lustighausen in order to return to his capital. When he regained his private apartments, he perceived, above the treetops, the glow of a fire. He called for his spyglass and saw that Traurighausen was burning. His dear Minette rushed in, upon hearing his cries. She seized the spyglass. At that moment, the roof of the château, undermined by the fire, collapsed. A black monster, of fantastic proportions, circled above the furnace, then flew away, leaving behind him a phosphorescent wake. The former nun uttered a terrible scream:

"I have seen the Devil!"

And she fell down stone dead.

The Chevalier d'Armel's Wedding

■ ■ ■ BY THE FOLLIES OF ITS PRINCES and the extravagance ■ ■ ■
of their entourage, the little Court of Effingen had acquired
for itself, by 1830, a reputation which was the astonishment of
Europe and the consternation of all Southern Germany.
While, in imitation of Weimar and Coburg, the taste for
belles-lettres or the cultivation of the milder virtues reigned in
most of the Germanic States, Effingen furnished an example
of the most shameful libertinage as well as of the wildest dis-
sipation. For over half a century, in fact, the Grand Ducal
House had virtually forsaken the obligations of power for the
frivolities of love and, according to their inclinations, the
Grand Dukes of Effingen eloped with shepherds or shepherd-
esses, actors or prima donnas, lackeys or ladies-in-waiting.

In alternation, the Academy of Pages and the *corps de ballet*
controlled the government. The former had been founded by
Grand Duke Ernst-August, who made terrible depredations
among its ranks, but his nephew, who preferred good-looking
women, had built the Opera and maintained the *corps de ballet*
on funds from his civil list.

Grand Duke Emmanuel III had restored the tradition of
his uncle Ernst-August and conferred new lustre on the Academy of Pages, which had been woefully neglected during the
preceding reign. Candidates were diligently screened, and His
Highness did not disdain visiting the establishment in person
to superintend the instruction that was given there. Corporal
punishment had been reinstated by his orders, and it was
whispered that he took a particular and personal pleasure in
witnessing its administration.

As he grew older, Grand Duke Emmanuel III had fallen into a profound aberration of both mind and senses. His subjects, who had hitherto patiently endured his debauches and their costly repercussions upon the public treasury, nearly rebelled when their master had raised to the dignity of titular favourite a Zanzibar Negro who had come in the retinue of an eccentric Lord. This nobleman, who travelled in order to distract his mind from an incurable melancholy, had bought the black boy from Barbary pirates and attached him to his train, amused by the contrasts of his own pallor, his blue eyes and blond curls, with the blackamoor's inky skin and kinky hair. He obliged the creature to follow him everywhere, like a tame animal. It was thus that the Grand Duke had first caught sight of him at a Court Ball. Instantly inflamed, he offered the Nubian's master three thousand florins if he would give him up. The Englishman, beguiled, had consented to the bargain and the Negro found himself accorded forthwith the most exceptional honours.

Not content with dressing him magnificently and building for him, within the palace grounds, a pavilion that resembled a mosque, Emmanuel III, completely distracted by passion, had desired to make the Nubian a Baron and oblige Effingen's nobility to accept him as one of themselves. The latter, justifiably outraged, had revolted. All the Barons of the Grand Duchy, forgetting their protocolary disputes, had joined forces and armed their peasants. This faction arrived one morning beneath the walls of the capital and camped there, screaming for the head of the former slave. Alarmed, Emmanuel III dismissed his favourite, who was forthwith cast into prison. This concession did not prevent the pillage of the oriental pavilion, and the Grand Duke's own residence narrowly escaped burning. Faced with this regrettable turn of events, Emmanuel III had taken refuge in some worthy's house, where, the next day, a delegation of the Barons came to negotiate with him. Old Baron d'Hochstadt, leader of this embassy, observed to his master that Effingen did not lack handsome boys who would be quite proud to be singled out by their sovereign, and he entreated the latter to cast his eyes upon them rather than upon foreigners, for that was an insult to his own subjects.

Chastened by this experience, the Grand Duke promised to choose his favourites among adventurers no longer, but to reserve this enviable post to the sons or the nephews of his loyal servitors. Everyone went home satisfied, and the Zanzibar Negro, the cause of the conflict, was sold to a circus passing through the capital.

At the period when this story begins, Emmanuel III had been confined, half mad, to his château at Lauterwill, in the heart of the mountains, and he was living there quite modestly, surrounded by a Court of young shepherds. Meanwhile, the Regency was assured by Privy Councillor von Klausser until Prince Karl-August should be old enough to assume the responsibilities of sceptre and crown. The Prince was only fifteen years of age, but already found himself the object of every form of lust, the focal point of every ambition.

Weary of the virtuous yoke which Councillor von Klausser's austere administration burdened them with, Court and capital alike were beginning to grow restive. The childhood of the heir presumptive was searched for clues of immorality that might justify certain hypotheses. Some recalled that the young Prince had manifested a tender predilection for one of his childhood companions and had wept at his departure. Others declared that he had been whipped by his tutor for kissing a chambermaid in a hallway of the palace. The uncertainty was considerable, and the two factions that divided Society opposed each other to obtain supremacy over the future Grand Duke. The faction of the Pages, as we may call it, supported by the Order of the Yellow Dragon and the English Ambassador, contended by intrigues against that of the Opera, backed by the Jesuits and the French Ambassador, whose pretty daughter

84

was its principal trump. It is true that the son of the British Ambassador was also richly provided with charms, and Fortune appeared to favour neither side above the other.

Shut up in his study, Privy Councillor von Klausser was brooding over the difficulties of the situation and over those of his task, when a loud commotion of carriage horses and oaths reached his ears and distracted him from his meditation. An inquisitive spirit by nature, he ran to the window. A magnificent equipage had stopped before his door. The carriage, a travelling barouche whose colour was concealed by a heavy layer of mud and dust, must have been of foreign origin, for never had the Councillor seen any as elegant in the Grand Duchy. His curiosity mounted when he saw a stranger get out of the vehicle and make for his own residence. He was delighted, for he enjoyed nothing so much as an unexpected visit. He hastily returned to his desk, picked up several papers and began to glance through them distractedly, impatient to have his visitor announced. He listened to the concussion of the knocker against the door, the creak the latter made as it opened and the footsteps of the lackey climbing the stairs to the study. Without even reading the name written in the cartouche, he recognized the armorial bearings engraved on the card presented to him. "My nephew!" he exclaimed, and rapidly ran down the stairs.

The nephew who had thus fallen from heaven was the only son of Councillor von Klausser's sister, an amiable and languishing lady whose sentimental adventures had formerly occupied the attention of the gazettes. Despite her family's opposition, she had married a French nobleman who had emigrated to Effingen, the Chevalier d'Armel, a man suspected, not without reason, of having already married in his own country. Nonetheless, upon the establishment of the Empire, the d'Armels had returned to France and the Councillor had never seen his sister again, for she had died of consumption shortly after the birth of her son. What in the world had this latter come to Effingen for? the Councillor wondered. Why hadn't he notified him of his visit beforehand?

As he walked into the salon, he found his visitor standing before a portrait that represented the Councillor in his Grand Chamberlain's robes. The young man was examining it carefully through his monocle, and this study absorbed him so deeply that he had not heard the model approach.

"Well now, my dear nephew, do you find me to your taste?"

"Ah, my uncle, be good enough to forgive me," the nephew replied, with a start. "I was attempting to conceive your character from the features of your countenance. . . ."

"Is it indiscreet to ask for your impression?"

"An excellent one, my uncle, excellent! I discern a generous heart that will sympathize with my misfortunes and help me to surmount them."

"Before listening to the account of your adversities, let me look at you, my dear boy. I was very fond of my sister, your mother, and I confess that I am quite moved to see how nearly you resemble her."

The Chevalier d'Armel, as a matter of fact, by dint of loving women and living on such intimate terms with them, had learnt from them certain manners which, combined with his quasi-feminine type of beauty, might have caused him to pass for less virile than he was in reality. He expressed himself in good German, but with a faint English accent that perfectly matched his *recherché* attire, the last word in London. Without waiting to be asked, he sat down in an armchair, crossed his legs and began his story in an easy tone:

"To keep nothing of the truth from you, I left Paris five days ago, following an unfortunate gaming incident. I was accused of cheating. Since that was the case," he said with a laugh, "I was obliged to deny the accusation indignantly. I slapped the insolent fellow, for that was the only means of protesting my innocence, and the next morning I killed him in a duel. Unfortunately the personage in question was very highly placed and had notified the police beforehand in the most cowardly fashion, stipulating that in case he failed to return alive, a warrant for my arrest was to be sworn out against me that very evening. In order to spare my family the shame of seeing me in prison, and my friends the drudgery of visiting me there, I crossed the frontier as rapidly as possible. . . . At first I knew not where to turn, and then it occurred to me to ask you for asylum and protection. Will you be good enough to take me in, my dear uncle?"

The Councillor was deeply embarrassed, which he did not conceal from his nephew. He consented to receive the young man only with the provision that he cause no uproar in the capital and breathe no word of this affair to anyone. The Chevalier promised everything his uncle asked of him, and even went so far as to swear that his future conduct would redeem that of his past. Having thereby assuaged his uncle's fears, he was free to give himself up to his habitual good humour, and made a thousand jokes concerning his own adversity. That evening, he enlivened the Councillor's table by remarks full of wit and spirit, and was pronounced charming by all.

Eight days later, he was the hero of fashion, and the entire capital was buzzing over the abominable machination of which he had been the victim. His pretty face and gallant manners won him the favour of every woman, and the cynical way in which he discussed them, the esteem of every man. His first successes gave him a good opinion of Effingen, and, because his satiated vanity inclined him to kindness, he declared everything to be perfect. His uncle had feared lest, accustomed to the brilliant salons of Paris, he might consider those of the Grand Duchy's capital quite lustreless, but, on the contrary, he seemed to take the liveliest pleasure in frequenting them. He was seen playing piquet with old Marshal d'Aberwitz, singing Italian airs at the *soirées* of the Baroness d'Hochstadt, improvising charades at the house of Councillor of State Firensius, pushing Mademoiselle Ludovica von Stomberg's swing, and even giving advice to Madame de Gurtennau as to the disposition of her garden. He was so taken up that he had scarcely leisure to be bored. His afternoons and evenings were given up to the *beau monde*, and only his mornings were his own, in which to read a little, write letters and visit the countryside. Despite his taste for Society, he enjoyed these solitary strolls, during which he could reflect at his ease upon his new position, savouring its charms and sinking into sweet daydreams over his future. It was impossible for him to sojourn much longer with his uncle. Where would he then take up residence? Of course, he had no money, but up until the present he had been able to meet his expenses, notably his gambling debts, by means of the sum realized on the sale of his carriage. The day it was exhausted, he would have to find a new expedient. Each morning the Chevalier was tormented by this problem, but the afternoon's pleasures made him forget his cares, and by evening he was cheerfully losing several more florins.

Only an affluent marriage could save him. He was indeed thinking seriously of such a thing, and already saw himself the owner of an agreeable country house two or three leagues from the capital, dividing his time between the education of his children, the management of his domain and some literary projects. The prospect enchanted him by its novelty and its idyllic character. After the disorderly life he had led in France, he dreamed, now, of playing another role, and that of Werther would not have displeased him, yet where to find a Charlotte? The tone of the society in which he had been received retained something of the eighteenth century and the influence of the *Philosophes*: its conversations were extremely free, and well-brought-up young ladies took no part in them. The Chevalier despaired of ever meeting any young woman in such company who might answer his needs and, in order to insure his future, he was contemplating a match with Madame de Gurtennau, a widow twenty years older than himself but extremely wealthy. Several times, apropos of the art of gardening, she had made urgent allusions to husbandry, seeking from her amateur landscape artist lessons of another sort altogether. The Chevalier had always turned a deaf ear to these requests and had been careful not to follow her into the bosky dells where, under various pretexts, she attempted to lead him. He had even refused to go to her house in the evening in order to examine the stars through a spyglass, for such astronomical zeal and the night's complicity promised nothing good. Was he to capitulate and yield himself up, body and soul, to the wealth of the ardent widow? This was the only path that opened before him, and he confided his plan to his uncle. The latter exclaimed in disparagement and attempted to show him the drawbacks of such a match.

"She is fearfully ugly and is twenty years older than you as well!"

"One never knows what a wife will become later on: I prefer to marry her at once. That way, at least, I shall have no unfortunate surprises."

"And you shall be assured of her fidelity. No one will steal her away from you!" the Councillor observed with a chuckle.

"That's just the trouble: who would try to take her off my hands?"

"Seriously, my boy, have you thought of the scandal such a union will provoke? You will lose at one and the same time your reputation and any chance of happiness. . . ."

"It is true that the ceremony will resemble a funeral more than a wedding, but when one is on the point of drowning one does not scruple to seize whatever log is closest. Besides, Madame de Gurtennau is not so ugly as all that, and the joy of remarrying will transfigure her!"

Nevertheless the Councillor begged his nephew to reflect further and not commit himself hastily. The Chevalier an-

swered that he would obey this request and ask for Madame de
Gurtennau's hand only in the last extremity, on the day he had
spent his final florin. The Councillor immediately gave him
some fifty, which afforded the Chevalier several weeks' respite.
Salvation offered itself quite opportunely a few days later, and
in another guise, infinitely more seductive, than that of Madame de Gurtennau.

One morning, as he was taking his customary stroll through
the countryside, the Chevalier d'Armel was diverted from his
reflections by a strange music that seemed to be coming from
within a large garden whose walls he was following. Surprised, he stopped in order to listen more closely. Someone was
playing the harpsichord, at random and without method, for
he could distinguish no theme, but he delighted in the music
for its very incoherence. With a single leap he reached the top
of the wall in order to see what was on the other side. A series
of geometric flowerbeds bordered by severe box hedges was
vouchsafed to his gaze, then a pond and, half hidden by trees,
a huge yellow house with green shutters. Here was the source
of the music which intrigued him so greatly. He would have
remained to contemplate the handsome residence longer had
not a lady of majestic aspect appeared on the threshold. She
stepped into a two-horse carriage that had just driven up. A
footman took his place beside the driver, and the equipage
trotted off while the Chevalier hastily scrambled down from
the wall in order not to be caught in the act of committing an
indiscretion. Having returned to his uncle's house, he asked
the latter if he knew to whom this fine residence belonged,
and thereby learned that it was the home of the Baroness Zimmerwegg, a widow of great distinction and considerable fortune. She had two daughters whom she was rearing strictly, in
the fear of God and men alike. The elder, Baroness Charlotte,
was possessed of a sensitive and dreamy nature. She loved
beautiful landscapes and wept when she read poetry. The
Councillor showed some astonishment that his nephew had

not already encountered her upon his rural walks, a book in her hand. The second daughter was studying Hebrew and spoke Greek with ease. As an exceptional privilege, the Academy of Effingen had opened its doors to her and, before an assemblage of delighted elders, she had read, with many blushes, an enthralling monograph on the Roman potteries recently discovered in the Grand Duchy. These details amused the Chevalier d'Armel. He asked his uncle if either one of these girls was fond of music. The Councillor informed him that to his knowledge neither one of the sisters played the harpsichord, but that perhaps the Baroness Charlotte, the better to translate the romantic exaltations of her soul, had given herself up to musical improvisations.

The following week, thanks to his new friends, the Chevalier managed to make the acquaintance of the Baroness Zimmerwegg, whom he plied with compliments. Enchanted by such amiability, she immediately invited him to her home, in order to present him to her daughters. His surprise was considerable upon seeing them, for he had imagined a tearful muse and a crabbed blue-stocking, whereas he saw before him two blonde, fresh young girls whose cheeks coloured quite prettily as they curtseyed to him. The Chevalier could not keep from admiring the whiteness of their arms, the delicacy of their hands, the fragile line of their necks, and the discreet palpitation of their throats. He dared not tell them so, lest he augment their already visible emotion, but his eager gallantry bore sufficient witness to his sentiments. A collation was served upon the terrace, and then the young Baronesses resumed their needlepoint, while the Chevalier conversed with their mother. The latter's remarks were in no way brilliant, though lively and full of good sense. The Chevalier took great pleasure in them, and since he was able to offer repartee on certain edifying subjects which he had almost never heard discussed, he was quite proud of his own manner. He was, moreover, a little weary of his libertinage, his frivolous life and his cynicism, and by becoming sensible of virtue, believed himself virtuous. This discovery astonished him agreeably, and upon taking leave of the Baroness he asked permission to return. After his departure the Zimmerweggs spoke highly of their visitor, and the young Baronesses discussed him at length that evening in their bedchamber.

Gradually, the Chevalier grew accustomed to visiting the Zimmerweggs regularly, at first every three or four days and soon daily, neglecting for their sake the salons of the Marschallin d'Aberwitz, of Baroness d'Hochstadt and Councillor of State Firensius, but these good souls forgave him his desertion, and indeed all Effingen society followed this idyll with interest, wondering which of the two sisters would triumph over the other. Councillor von Klausser was most pleased of all by this turn of events, for he saw in it, for his nephew, a prospect of establishment, and in order to accelerate matters, he sang the young man's praises to anyone who would listen. The obscure and sinister affair that had obliged him to leave Paris so hastily became, in the Councillor's mouth, a monstrous judicial error. It was thus that, for the love of a Frenchman, the sentiments of Effingen's nobility became ardently anti-French.

Happy in his popularity and in the interest he aroused, the Chevalier d'Armel found life a delightful proposition. He spent the major portion of his days in the large yellow house with green shutters, where he had made himself indispensable. He helped the Baroness keep her accounts, put the library in order and, after meals, played reversi or backgammon with her. The rest of the time he went riding with the Baroness Charlotte or herborized in the meadows with her sister. On occasion, they were joined by friends: the young people would crowd together in a large *char-à-banc* and set off to visit some picturesque site in the vicinity. The Baroness Charlotte sketched it in her album or recited a poem inspired by the occasion, then they sat quite unceremoniously upon the grass to eat a cold repast: rustic pleasures whose innocence charmed the Chevalier's heart. . . . The days and the weeks thus passed by without his taking a moment's notice. At the beginning of autumn, intoxicated by this sentimental atmosphere, he asked for the hand of the Baroness Charlotte. The news would have comprised the principal subject of all conversation, if another event had not distracted the capital's attention.

The young Prince Karl-August, in whose behalf Councillor von Klausser exercised the Regency, fell ill of a mortal fever and perished. Consternation was widespread in the Grand Duchy, for the Prince was the House of Effingen's last male heir. Upon his demise, the throne reverted to his elder sister, the Princess Marie-Thérèse. This alteration in the order of succession ruined the plans of the Academy of Pages and those of the Opera faction alike, and both establishments flew their flags at half-mast. It was only the common people who rejoiced, for they supposed that a woman's reign would be more liberal and her despotism gentler, in which they were guilty of a grave error.

The Princess Marie-Thérèse possessed several of those strong and virile virtues which characterize the great sovereigns. Unsociable by nature, inclined towards mistrust, she had appeared only rarely at the Court, devoting the major part of her activity to the Chase. She had reduced the number of her ladies-in-waiting to increase that of her huntsmen; her chambermaids had been replaced by beaters; and she generally held audience in her stables, while superintending the grooming of the horses. She rode, shot and swam like a man. Her entourage had no special fondness for her, but *bizarreries* of character being common among the Effingens, no one dreamed of showing surprise at the Princess's tastes. She had, further, a highly developed sense of authority which boded no good.

The first session of the Crown Council was a stormy one. Councillor von Klausser found himself asked to resign, whereas he had expected to retain his responsibilities at least semi-officially. The celebrations of the coronation dissipated the last doubts that might have obscured the new Grand Duchess's intentions. No sooner had she assumed the hereditary crown than she announced her decision to govern entirely by herself and to raise Effingen to the first rank among the Germanic powers. She demanded an augmentation of the already heavy taxes and an increase in statute-labour. Consequently when she passed through the capital on the day of the ceremony ovations were few and far between.

The regime's first days confirmed the fears of the people. The army's forces were doubled, as were the taxes. A further assessment was levied to create a war fleet on Lake Narvels, and Councillor von Klausser was appointed its Admiral. This unexpected dignity consoled him for being Regent no longer. He took his functions quite seriously and henceforth spent his time on a small sloop which shot across the lake in all directions, causing great commotion among the fishermen and damaging their nets. No longer having the leisure to sit on the Crown Council, Admiral von Klausser transmitted his charge to his nephew, and it was in this manner that the Chevalier began to play a part in the Grand Duchy's affairs.

His political accomplishments did not dazzle his colleagues, but, on the other hand, his beauty produced a profound impression upon the Grand Duchess, who granted him a private audience without his having dreamed of soliciting this favour, albeit one so warmly sought after. During this interview, he enlivened the Sovereign's mood by wittily describing to her the intrigues of her courtiers, and this was the beginning of his dizzying ascent in the administrative hierarchy, and official honours as well. Having been appointed Grand Chamberlain, then Councillor of War and Master of the Hunt, he obtained, several months later, the coveted post of Court Marshal. This sudden favour enchanted the Baroness Zimmerwegg and her daughters, but since the Chevalier, absorbed by his new tasks, came to see them less frequently, they eventually conceived a certain vexation at the scarcity of his visits and took umbrage at their Sovereign's new predilection. What irritated them most were the signs of the Chevalier's evident satisfaction. He showed a smiling face at the doors of gala carriages, received foreign ambassadors beside the Grand Duchess, and in short reigned discreetly, with affability and good grace.

One day, while the Sovereign was riding in a barouche to one of her summer residences, the Chevalier, who was galloping alongside the coach as the demands of etiquette decreed, fell from his horse and dislocated his wrist. The Grand Duchess immediately ordered her carriage to stop and insisted that the afflicted horseman be placed inside it, next to her. The following day Court and capital alike were gossiping about the incident. The Baroness Zimmerwegg, to whom, not without a certain perfidy, the news had been brought first, fell into a Biblical rage and took council with her daughters. They resolved to consider the betrothal as broken and dispatched to the faithless lover the presents he had given to the Baroness Charlotte. Afterwards the Baroness Zimmerwegg appeared in the salons of the capital and loudly criticized the Grand Duchess's tasteless deportment. That same evening, an officer, with an escort of soldiers, presented himself at her residence and, despite her vehement protests, caused her and her daughters to be taken to an old fortress which afforded an extremely clear view over Lake Narvels. The three ladies were imprisoned there without further ado. This summary behaviour, which revealed both the passion and the jealousy of the Grand Duchess, astounded Effingen society, yet no one presumed to reveal his astonishment. The Chevalier himself dared say nothing. The Academy of Pages faction took advantage of this situation to raise its head, and since it could scarcely advance the candidacy of one of its own members, decided to support the new favourite's career. The Opera party took the contrary position, of course, and assumed the task of defending the Grand Duchess's virtue. It dispatched to her a Jesuit Father, who offered a number of respectful remonstrances mingled with theological and historical arguments. The Sovereign dismissed him coolly enough, though she received in the same insouciant fashion the French Ambassador, who permitted himself several observations upon her conduct. A few hours later the official demand for his recall had been sent off to Paris, attended to by the Chevalier himself.

The latter, in truth, while thanking Heaven for his good fortune, was alarmed by the price at which he would have to pay for it. The Grand Duchess, if she had a man's firm and virile character, had also certain other masculine qualities: a deep voice, made somewhat husky by the duties of command (for she directed the manœuvres of her regiment herself), an upper lip darkened by a downy moustache which the Court painters could scarcely neglect without losing the resemblance, and finally a brusque, imperative manner entirely lacking in feminine grace. Frequently the Chevalier recalled, with a tinge of regret, how the Baroness Charlotte used to read aloud so harmoniously, or the charming way in which she concealed her embarrassment behind her needlework, when he made her some more than ordinarily lively compliment. If, out of pure courtliness, he behaved in this wise with the Grand Duchess, the latter shrugged her shoulders or replied:

"Do you take me for a witless flirt? Don't play the courtier with me, *mon cher*! You please me enough without that. . . ."

On each such occasion, the Chevalier, thus rebuked, felt himself at a loss and dissimulated his embarrassment by signing some decree or silently annotating a document to submit to his Sovereign's approbation. Indeed, the pair worked together constantly. The Chevalier had become a kind of Prime Minister: nothing could now be effected without consulting him first. The Crown Council had been, if not dissolved, at least deposed from power and stripped of the majority of its prerogatives. The Grand Duchess was quite unaffected by its advice and did not trouble to seek it when she resolved to marry the Chevalier d'Armel. She merely announced her decision to the House of Lords in which the representatives of the Nobility sat.

The news caused little surprise but a great deal of emotion. In general, the Sovereign was reproached for this misalliance, and, in agreement for once, the Opera faction and that of the Academy of Pages decided that it would have been preferable, for the Crown's lustre, that the Grand Duchess take the Chevalier as a lover rather than a husband. None the less, the opposition, rendered discreet by the imprisonment of the Baroness Zimmerwegg and her daughters, offered no reaction, the prospect of the wedding celebrations sufficing to occupy everyone's mind.

A few days after this event, the Grand Duchess, in a colonel's black-and-red uniform, a tricorne on her head and a crop in her hand, was reviewing her troops when her horse, startled by the sudden "Viva!" of a drunken soldier, reared and threw the Sovereign from the saddle. Two *aides-de-camp* rushed up to offer succour. The Grand Duchess did not appear to be hurt, but the liveliest agitation was painted upon her countenance.

"To the palace, quickly!" she murmured.

No sooner had she returned to her apartments than she dismissed her maids, her lady-in-waiting and all those who hovered about her, declaring she had need of no one. She desired only to be left in peace in order to recover from the alarm she had suffered. The next day, the *Effingen Gazette*, after relating the incident, added that the Grand Duchess would keep to her bedchamber for several days. This news would have had nothing astonishing about it had the Sovereign's singular attitude not cast a veil of mystery over an event that intrigued the familiars of the palace. No one, indeed, was admitted to her private apartments, with the exception of the footman who served her meals. Ministers, physicians, chaplain, chamberlains—everyone, including the Chevalier d'Armel and the

Grand Duchess's own sister, the Princess Wilhelmine, was scrupulously excluded. Nevertheless, she continued to concern herself with affairs of State and received the diplomatic courier regularly. Most alarming was the fact that, though unwilling to be ministered to, she declared herself to be an invalid still, and refused to leave her bed. Then, one fine day, she sent for an illustrious physician from Vienna, who spent the better part of an afternoon at her bedside. He confined himself to declaring, upon taking his leave, that there was no cause to fear for the Sovereign's health. This laconism disconcerted the Court, which immediately gave itself up to a thousand suppositions, all injurious to the Grand Duchess's virtue. No one doubted further that she was with child, and the Chevalier was frequently the object of ironic congratulations, though he vainly protested his innocence.

A month later the situation had not changed. The Grand Duchess now claimed that her nerves had been unsettled; the footman who served her reported that she was living in semi-darkness and wore a great black veil over her head—to relieve her migraines, she said. It was in this garb that the Chevalier d'Armel found her one day, when, in a paroxysm of anxiety, he had forced her door. At the sound of his footsteps, a harsh voice had cried out: "Who's there?" with such vehemence that he had stopped on the threshold, fearing to be shot point-blank by some sentry. Then, upon a fresh challenge, he mustered up his courage and groped his way through the room.

"It is I, madame, the Chevalier d'Armel. . . . I took the liberty of coming in. . . . I was so distressed!"

The voice softened somewhat:

"I am glad it is you, Chevalier, sit down. I intended, as a matter of fact, to have you sent for, for I wished to discuss a matter of the greatest importance with you."

The Chevalier took a stool and waited. After one or two moments of silence, the Sovereign's voice rose again, this time with a tender inflection:

"Do you still love me, Chevalier?"

"Ah, madame, more than ever! If such a thing were possible. My love and my anxiety are forever contending in Your Highness's behalf. . . ."

"May I, then, rely on your absolute devotion?"

"I belong, body and soul, to Your Highness. She may dispose of me as she pleases."

"Well, then, *mon cher*, I am going to give you a proof of love and devotion in my turn: I have decided to sacrifice my throne and to abdicate in order to devote myself to you altogether. Were it to be otherwise, the obligations of power would prevent me from doing so."

These words overwhelmed the Chevalier. He blessed the darkness and his interlocutress's veil, which permitted him to conceal his perplexity. In a deeply moved and persuasive tone, he opposed this project, insinuating that he would consider himself responsible for this abdication in the eyes of History, that the judgment of posterity alarmed him, and that furthermore the happiness of the Grand Duchess's subjects should take precedence over his own. His Sovereign listened to this discourse with agitation and did not conceal the displeasure it caused her.

"I am free to act as I please, Monsieur le Chevalier. My decision is irrevocable. I am not unaware that I am detested by my people and that they will be delighted to be rid of me. I shall yield the crown to my sister, the Princess Wilhelmine, who will certainly succeed in this difficult task better than I have been able to do. She is kind, gentle, prudent and pretty. No one will regret me."

"Ah, madame, Your Highness must not say such things. All the Court is plunged into desolation, ever since this strange malady. . . ."

And the Chevalier fell silent, confused. He saw the position of Prince Consort escaping him, and the prospect of uniting his fate with that of a dethroned Grand Duchess was scarcely

an alluring one. All his calculations collapsed in consequence
of this unexpected decision whose motives he tried in vain to
fathom. The Sovereign's illness must have unsettled her mind.
He already envisaged the possibility of having her examined
by a council of physicians, when his future bride, perhaps divining his thoughts, said to him:

"Do not suppose I have gone mad. I have long and carefully
considered my new situation, and for my repose, as for my
honour, it is advisable that I withdraw from the throne."

"What situation, madame?" asked the Chevalier, puzzled.

"The one in which my brother's death has placed me," she
replied with a slight gesture of impatience. "I am not made to
govern human beings. This task is beyond my strength. During this malady I have had time for reflection, and I have realized, Chevalier, that only one thing merits our attention. . . ."

"And what is that, madame?"

"To assure our eternal salvation!"

"Heavens!"

"Do not argue, *mon cher*. All my arrangements have been
made, and even the site of our retreat has been chosen. We
shall leave the palace tomorrow, after dark. In the meantime,
you will bring man's clothing for me, in order that I may not
be recognized, or even suspected. We shall have left the Grand
Duchy before our departure is even noticed."

"But why so much mystery, madame? Will you not even bid
your subjects farewell?"

"No, I wish to leave in the greatest secrecy. Do not forget
that I am eloping with you! We shall thus be obeying the best
romantic traditions. Moreover, I shall leave instructions with
my Chancellor so that my succession is accomplished without
any disorder. Since you are here, sit down at that desk and
write as I tell you."

The Grand Duchess dictated several messages, instructions
to her ministers and a farewell letter to the Princess Wilhelmine. When this task was completed, she dismissed the
Chevalier:

"I count on you, therefore, to accompany me. You have just sworn your obedience and loyalty: now is the moment to keep your promises!"

The Chevalier thought he discerned a trace of mockery in these words. Was the Grand Duchess speaking seriously, or did she wish to test him?

And since he said nothing, all perplexed as he was, she continued:

"Come now, Chevalier, submit with good grace! You will have nothing to regret, I assure you. . . . Besides, remember that I am still all-powerful here. In case you should attempt to steal away, I shall have you arrested."

The Chevalier d'Armel, sick at heart, did as he was bid and took the necessary measures to prepare for their flight. The Grand Duchess still wore her veil over her head and appeared profoundly afflicted, despite the timbre of her voice which was sterner than ever. The Chevalier was amazed that she should be in a state to undertake this journey. He observed as much to his Sovereign, but she declared that she felt better already and that the change of air would do her good.

Everything proceeded as the Grand Duchess had foreseen. At the appointed hour the Grand Duchess joined him in a barouche waiting for her at the far end of the palace grounds, behind a small unguarded gate. He helped her to her seat and took his own beside her, abashed at this escapade of whose outcome he was still in ignorance. They rode all night long, stopping only to change horses. The Grand Duchess, sensitive to the cold, had wrapped herself from head to feet in a travelling cloak; she responded only in monosyllables to the Chevalier, who plied her with questions as to the circumstances of her flight from the palace. She finally went to sleep and her companion, nonplussed, did the same in order to forget, however fleetingly, his perplexities. They were awakened at dawn by the necessities of crossing the frontier. The Chevalier exhibited his own passport and that of the Grand Duchess, made out in the name of "Count von Pfannenstiel, Lieutenant in the

Empress's Regiment, returning to Vienna". The border official, impressed by the rank of the barouche's occupants, let them pass without hindrance, and the barouche took the road for Vienna at a fast trot. At about ten in the morning, the Grand Duchess emerged from her somnolence. She threw off her cloak, stretched, and removed the hat which she had kept on her head all night long. At this moment a sunbeam lit up her face; an exclamation of astonishment burst from the Chevalier: it was not the ex-Sovereign who was sitting beside him, but a man! No doubt it was the real Count von Pfannenstiel. The latter, observing the Chevalier's bewilderment, could not restrain a smile.

"You don't recognize me, *mon cher*?"

"No, monsieur, and I find this joke in the worst of taste. What have you done with Her Highness?"

"Really, you don't recognize me? Now look at me carefully!"

Amazed, the Chevalier considered the Lieutenant closely. Gradually an idea which he considered absurd dawned upon him. This man, incontestably, resembled the Grand Duchess! He had the same cold grey eyes, the same strong and wilful mouth, the same somewhat arched nose. What did this mean? Indeed, that beard, those badly trimmed moustaches did not seem to be false, and the stranger's voice was certainly that of the Grand Duchess when she had exclaimed, "Who's there!" the day he had entered her bedchamber unexpectedly.

"For Heaven's sake, monsieur, put an end to my uncertainty! What is the meaning of this substitution?"

"Ah, Chevalier, you will not believe me, for the truth sometimes surpasses all credence. I am—or rather I was—the Grand Duchess Marie-Thérèse!"

"What, monsieur . . . madame, I mean . . . it cannot be possible!"

"Yet it is! I was the Grand Duchess until that day I fell from my horse. . . . When I came to myself, I had become a man.

This transformation overwhelmed me with stupefaction; I dared not announce it to my Court. I therefore attempted to keep the secret of this news as long as possible, not knowing what decision to take. Consider my perplexity! Then I summoned from Vienna that physician who could only bow before the evidence. After having despaired of what to do, I reached the conclusion that this event was, after all, providential. An ugly and a graceless Princess, I was now transformed into a rather handsome man, is it not so?"

"Indeed it is, Highness, but I assure you that you were not . . ."

"No more compliments, *mon cher*. I now wish to take the best advantage of this metamorphosis, and in order to do so it must remain unknown: otherwise I could never live in peace and would become merely an object of curiosity for all of Europe. I trust my subjects will recognize my sister as their new Sovereign and will forget their former one, who can travel the world over without taking further thought for them. I have chosen a name for myself beneath which no one will divine my true identity. . . . Ah, Chevalier, how happy I am!"

With these words, Count von Pfannenstiel threw himself into his interlocutor's arms. The Chevalier associated himself with this joy without altogether sharing it. His memory quickly resuscitated strange accounts he had heard concerning the behavior of certain Grand Dukes of Effingen. The longer the carriage drove on, the greater his discomfort grew at travelling *tête-à-tête* with the Count. It was, indeed, the first time he had eloped with a Lieutenant, and he was eager to reach Vienna in order to extricate himself from this extraordinary situation. But, once there, what would they do? In any case, he was firmly resolved to rid himself of his companion by whatever means, should the latter prove too enterprising. The Chevalier watched him out of the corner of his eye and contrived to draw his attention to the various aspects of the landscape, in order not to leave his mind unoccupied. His relief was considerable when, at the post inn where they took luncheon, he noticed that Count von Pfannenstiel greedily scrutinized the waitresses who bustled about them. Indeed, the Count even permitted himself to make several reflections which the Chevalier found out of place from the lips of a former Grand Duchess.

In Vienna, the Count informed the Chevalier that he granted him his liberty, on the sole condition that he keep silence forever concerning this strange adventure. He obliged him to take an oath upon the Cross. Both men decided on an official version that would be made public in Effingen: the Grand Duchess had taken refuge in a convent in order to forget the world and dedicate herself to God. At the moment of their parting, Count von Pfannenstiel presented to the Chevalier d'Armel a case sealed with the Arms of the Grand Duchy.

"These are the last decrees I signed before renouncing the Crown. The first concerns the Baroness Zimmerwegg and her daughters; I command that they be restored their liberty. The second is your nomination to the rank of Colonel in my private regiment; you will replace me at its head: this is a favour always reserved for a member of the Grand Ducal family. The third is a certificate of hereditary rank as Count, on condition that you assume the glorious name of the Zimmerweggs, which otherwise would fall to the distaff side. I was not unaware of your betrothal to the Baroness Charlotte, and I intend that all these distinctions should make you forget the obstacles I once raised between the two of you."

The Chevalier burst into expressions of gratitude and protested his attachment to his former Sovereign.

"Let us not speak of such things any further," the Count replied, "and let us separate here as two friends. Continue to watch over the destiny of my country and advise my sister to the best of your ability. . . ."

Deeply moved by this peripety, the Chevalier returned to the barouche and without further delay took the road back to

Effingen. He was eager to release the Zimmerwegg family from prison and to enjoy his friends' stupefaction. The return journey seemed rapid to him, preoccupied as he was by the recollection of these recent events. He had broken the seals of the case, and never tired of reading the parchments that made him into one of the most important personages of the Grand Duchy.

When he arrived in the capital the following day, after having driven all night long, he was greeted by a great agitation caused by the Grand Duchess's disappearance and by his own. He attempted to furnish an explanation, but before he had even opened his mouth he was indignantly accused of having murdered the Grand Duchess. Despite his protests, he replaced the Zimmerweggs in their fortress, and the papers he was carrying on his person were seized. He insisted that they be examined at once, certain of them proving his innocence, but the members of the Crown Council declared they did not recognize the Sovereign's handwriting, which had been modified as a result of her own transformation. The letters which the Grand Duchess had dictated to him before leaving her palace were so many more charges against him. He was accused of having fabricated all these documents himself, and since he had made many envious enemies at the Court, he was not treated with any consideration. Councillor von Klausser himself believed him to be guilty and refused to defend his nephew before the Crown Council. The latter condemned him to decapitation, The date of the execution was immediately fixed for the following week. The people showed great joy at this event, for spectacles of such an order were becoming rare in Effingen.

While in the central square the stands from which the new Grand Duchess and the Court would witness the execution were being erected, the sad hero of this ceremony, after having penned a dignified letter to the Baroness Charlotte who had forsaken him, wrote yet another to the Grand Duchess Wilhelmine in order to reveal the whole truth to her and to ask for her reprieve. He entrusted both missives to his jailer, and to make certain of the man's loyalty gave him what few florins he had left. This largesse had an altogether different effect from the one which he had hoped to produce. Delighted by the windfall, the man drank himself senseless in the nearest wine-shop and completely forgot to dispatch the letters to their consignees. When he attempted to repair this neglect, two or three days later, he feared drawing attention to his negligence thereby, and kept the letters. As for the Chevalier, who was first astonished, then in despair at not receiving a reply, the jailer assured him quite brazenly that he had indeed carried out the commission with which he had been charged. When it came time to take the wretched Chevalier to the place of his final agony, the jailer slipped the letters into the pocket of a coat the prisoner had left upon his chair, thinking that in this way no one could suspect him of the slightest complicity. Delighted with the way in which he had disengaged himself from his dilemma, he gaily clanged shut the door of the prison and ran to join the crowd in the square.

The scaffold was magnificent, hung with crimson velvet, and on the block was to be seen a cushion embroidered with the arms of the d'Armel family. Immediately opposite stood the Court grandstand, protected from the sun by a great red-and-white striped canopy. The Grand Duchess Wilhelmine, for whom this was to be a first public appearance, was enthroned among her intimates in all the brilliance of her eighteen years and a diamond aigrette. The entire Court was there, with the exception of Councillor von Klausser, whose sense of propriety had forbade him to attend. But the Baroness Zimmerwegg, pale from her sojourn in the fortress, looked forward to the punishment of the impious regicide with a satisfaction she made no attempt to conceal. The young Baronesses had remained at home, for their mother had decided, not without reason, that this was no spectacle for sensitive souls. Among the crowd, a good number of old soldiers and disabled

veterans were to be noticed, wrecks of the Napoleonic con-
scription, who noisily manifested their delight at seeing a
Frenchman in the pillory. The Court, on the contrary, seemed
to relent as the minutes passed. The Chevalier had such an interesting expression, with his magnificent royal-blue suit and
his yellow waistcoat. Such elegance touched Society's heart.

"What a pity to put to death a man who has such good
taste!" said Mademoiselle Ludovica von Stomberg.

"And one who is so handsome!" added Madame de Gurtennau mournfully.

And these two ladies heaved deep sighs, fluttering their fans
while a herald read out the sentence. At this moment, a coach-
and-four drove into a corner of the square and stopped,
impeded by the populace, but the latter, recognizing the arms
and the livery of the Court, made way to let the equipage pass.
This unexpected arrival distracted the attention of the Sovereign and of her entourage. Their astonishment reached its
height when they saw emerging from the carriage old Grand
Duke Emmanuel III, who seemed no less amazed than they.

"Well, well! What is going on here? I was on my way to
the palace, and they told me the Grand Duchess was in
the square. . . . Why all these people? Is there to be a
performance?"

A chamberlain hastily climbed down from the grandstand
to greet the old Monarch and to help him up to a seat. The
Grand Duke followed him, grumbling:

"Now then, Wilhelmine, what does all this mean? Where is
your sister?"

Upon the grandstand, the profoundest embarrassment was
allied with the most violent agitation. Everyone had quite forgotten the existence of Emmanuel III, and not a soul had
thought of informing him of the events that had occurred in
Effingen.

"My sister has been assassinated, and the murderer is to be
executed," the Grand Duchess replied peevishly.

She found this arrival highly inopportune, fearing that some scandal might result from it. The news of his granddaughter's disappearance produced no visible effect upon the Grand Duke, who sat down beside Wilhelmine and cast a number of triumphant glances upon the crowd before him. This scrutiny finished, he looked up and beheld the Chevalier, who, in the greatest distress imaginable, was wondering at the reason for this effervescence. For a moment he had comforted himself with the wild hope that the carriage might have brought the Count von Pfannenstiel, who had come thus in order to proclaim his innocence. The Chevalier's disappointment had been great when an old man he had never seen before descended from the vehicle.

"Now by God! There is a prisoner who has an interesting face!" the Grand Duke exclaimed, seizing his granddaughter's lorgnette, and he began to examine every detail of the Chevalier's person, emitting a series of appreciative little clucks. The scandal the Grand Duchess had feared occurred. Already the Court was amused by the old libertine's enthusiasm.

"I shall never believe this man is guilty," Emmanuel III continued. "What grace! What pride! He is certainly innocent . . . with such eyes! And a pretty mouth that could never lie. . . . I shall question him myself. My child," he said, turning towards his granddaughter, "have the condemned man brought to me. I wish to ask him some questions."

"But, Grandfather; you are mistaken. . . . This man is a criminal, unworthy of the least interest. . . . He has odiously done away with my poor sister. I implore you, do nothing of the kind: you will only disturb everyone!"

"To think I should be forced to hear such a thing, Wilhelmine! Do you dare disobey me? You forget that I ruled this country for over thirty years, and I intend that my wishes should still be respected. Baron," he continued, addressing himself to the Baron d'Hochstadt, "go get that boy for me. . . ."

Hesitating, the Baron glanced at the Grand Duchess, who did not wince. He painfully climbed down from the grandstand, crossed the square amid the most attentive silence, and commanded the soldiers on duty near the scaffold to escort the prisoner to the Grand Duke. The latter, quivering like an old coquette, reassured the Chevalier and asked him to tell his story as frankly as possible. Although astonished by the Grand Duke's behaviour, the Chevalier did not wait to be asked again. Profiting by this opportunity *in extremis*, he told the old monarch in the minutest details the circumstances which had brought him to the place of his execution. When Emmanuel III learned that his granddaughter had become a man, he burst out laughing.

"My God! How strange a tale! But it pleases me to include among my descendants one more male member of the line. All these girls were merely an insult to my reputation. Continue, my friend, continue," he said, pressing the Chevalier's hand.

The latter recounted his return to Effingen and the accusations that had been lodged against him, describing how he had been thrown into prison, and reproached the Grand Duchess for not having replied to his letter. Deeply disturbed by this declaration, she told him she had never received it. Since her word could scarcely be doubted, the Chevalier immediately shifted his suspicion to the feckless jailer. Two *aides-de-camp* were dispatched to find him and dragged him forward, trembling from head to foot. He confessed his negligence, and the Grand Duchess felt her heart stop beating at the thought that she had involuntarily been about to execute an innocent man. She rested upon the Chevalier, in order to solicit his pardon, a gaze as charming as it was distressed. The Grand Duke, for his part, exulted, and when the Chevalier had finished his story, embraced him impetuously.

"Ah, my son, my dear child—I may give you this title, since you owe your life to me—what a dreadful story! But what joy for me to have rescued you so adroitly. . . . There are certain presentiments that never lead one astray: no sooner had I seen you than . . ."

"Grandfather," the Grand Duchess interrupted, eager to restrain the old man's enthusiasm, "don't you think we had better return to the palace?"

"An excellent idea, my dear child. You, Chevalier, come with me. You shall accompany me in my carriage."

Once back at the palace, the Chevalier D'Armel, having recovered from his emotions, received the congratulations of the courtiers and explained several obscure points of his narrative. When he had finished, the Grand Duke Emmanuel III, whose eyes had never left him, exclaimed:

"There must be a moral to this adventure. Chevalier, our House has wronged you gravely. In order to offer reparation, I ask you to accept the hand of my granddaughter Wilhelmine. Were you not to have wed her sister? You can only gain by the exchange, and I shall settle down near the two of you. I was growing weary of that distant château to which I had been banished, and the solitude was beginning to hang heavy on my hands. You have no objections, Wilhelmine, if I return to the Court?"

The gallant Emmanuel III was beside himself with joy at the idea of ending his days in the company of so charming a grandson-in-law. . . . The young Grand Duchess acquiesced to these several projects. The wedding was celebrated several weeks later, amid general rejoicing. Reconciled, the faction of the Academy of Pages and that of the Opera offered the young couple a spectacle on the occasion which symbolized their new *entente*. Upon the Opera stage, a young page and a ballerina danced a ballet composed by Councillor of State Firensius. Its success was overwhelming, and it was necessary to restrain the Grand Duke, who, after having thrown his granddaughter's bouquet to the young artists, most vehemently desired to congratulate them in person.

In the course of time the Grand Duchess Wilhelmine presented her husband with six boys, each handsomer than the next, and the royal pair lived long enough to be driven from their thrones by a revolution.

Iphigenia in Thuringia

■ ■ ■ CERTAIN SOULS, too lofty to yield to their passions but ■ ■ ■ too ardent to abandon them, hesitate their entire existence between the heart's inclinations and the mind's demands; and if they ever bring themselves to make a choice, their decision is discovered to be more fatal than their previous uncertainty. Such was the destiny of Mademoiselle Iphigénie de Seewiesen, who after having carried the excesses of reason to the point of denying all merit to sentiment, fell in love late in life with a being unworthy of herself, and thereat died of affliction.

Until her thirtieth year Mademoiselle de Seewiesen, who owed her given name to her father's pronounced taste for Greek Antiquity, was considered one of the finest matches in the Holy Roman Empire and even in all of Europe. For a long time offers of marriage arrived in droves at the Château of Weissendorf, where she lived sequestered from a world she refused to know save by atlases, books and statues. Study appeared to be her only pleasure: she spent whole days in her library, and left it only in the evening, in order to observe the stars. A footman installed a spyglass upon the highest turret of the château, and here Mademoiselle de Seewiesen, disdaining the frivolous conversation of her father's guests, calculated the conjunctions of the heavenly bodies. Occasionally she was to be seen walking through the countryside, followed by a servant carrying a large green box. She advanced, her gait lively and supple, a plaited straw bonnet on her head to shield her from the sun; in one hand she held a botanical treatise, in the other a kind of long-handled trowel which she employed to press the high growths out of her way and to indicate to the servant those plants to be culled: it was in this fashion that Mademoiselle de Seewiesen herborized.

There was no science whose elements her encyclopaedic mind had not assimilated, no art in which her varied talents had not found means to display themselves. Empress Maria Theresa had invited her to Schoenbrunn to paint the Archduchess's portrait, and the King of Prussia had proposed that she take up residence in Potsdam in order to reign there over the wits of his Court. When she sat down at the clavier, her touch was proclaimed unrivalled; when she sang one of those arias she composed as a diversion from more austere activities, no one dared breathe for fear of clouding the purity of her voice. She danced to perfection, spoke French, English and Italian fluently, not to mention Greek and Latin, which she had mastered with a grace that was as effortless as it was untutored. As for mathematics, from her earliest years this science was so familiar to her that there was no problem whose solution she could not discover, a fact which confounded the most illustrious savants of the age. Religion was virtually the only subject towards which her rationalist spirit had not revealed the least inclination. Having been unable to explain God by algebra or chemistry, she ceased to believe in Him and contented herself with honouring the classical divinities to whom her friends compared her.

Such a wonder was not made for the lustreless life of Thuringia, and her father urged her to settle in Vienna or Paris in order to enjoy there the brilliant society that clamoured for her presence. Ever since a Prince of the House of Hanover, at the mere sight of her portrait, had asked for her hand, the most ambitious hopes appeared warranted, and Monsieur de Seewiesen often leafed through the *Almanach de Gotha*, flattering himself that one day perhaps his daughter would take her place in the chapter of the Sovereign Households. To these fond plans, unfortunately, Mademoiselle de Seewiesen refused to subscribe. The new Iphigenia did not appear at all eager to immolate herself for the sake of her father's vanity and considered the solitude of Weissendorf preferable to all the sumptuous establishments envisaged for her. It is true that this solitude was occupied by labours whose importance constituted the admiration of Europe. She maintained a regular correspondence with the most eminent of her contemporaries, which made her the best-informed person in the world. A Cardinal prepared, for her eyes alone, the secret chronicles of the Vatican; several Ministers of foreign Courts made no important decision without first soliciting her opinion; Archduke Lamprecht had chosen her as his Spiritual Mistress, and Archduchess Ottilie called her the Light of her Life. Goethe sent her his manuscripts and requested hers in return, beseeching her to join him at Weimar, where Duke Karl-August was dying with impatience to see her. Sir Horace Walpole, faithless to the memory of Madame du Deffand, wrote her letters that were almost passionate. In short, the élite of ten countries had their eyes fixed upon her, and King Louis XVI himself was no exception to the interest showered on this prodigious creature, for he invited her to Versailles.

Oblivious of these appeals, Mademoiselle de Seewiesen persisted in remaining at Weissendorf, which had become a second Ferney, to which visitors flocked. When she reached her thirtieth year, she declared formally that she would never marry, and requested that no one distract a retreat which she would consecrate entirely to Knowledge.

An English Duke, who had set out to effect her conquest, learned this news one evening, at a post inn. In his chagrin, he swore to marry the first woman he should see, and found himself thereby obliged to elope with the chambermaid of the inn, who became a Peeress of the Realm. A most illustrious Count of Königsegg-Haulenburg fell into so great a melancholy that his reason was despaired of and he had to be confined. The Prince Regent of Sonnenwalden had the portrait of Mademoiselle de Seewiesen placed in the throne room, on the armchair reserved for the future Princess, and the Gentlemen of his Court were henceforth obliged to make their obeisances to the effigy, since the model had disdained to occupy its place. Several young people of lesser rank spoke of suicide, but managed to console themselves with one actress or another. Many, nevertheless, refused to marry, for the image of the beautiful Iphigénie remained sole mistress of their hearts. It was only men of letters who rejoiced at her decision, for they feared lest marriage extinguish this star, or that it might be less brilliant should it gravitate into the orbit of some sovereign.

Henceforth, Mademoiselle de Seewiesen lived in an isolation that was almost complete. She ceased to appear at the nobility's balls, refused her neighbours' invitations, reduced her own hospitality to the very limits of propriety. She no longer left her library, and it was rumoured that she was writing a novel whose fame would equal if not surpass that of *La Nouvelle Héloïse*. The expectations of her admirers were not disappointed, for the success of this first work exceeded the most optimistic predictions. Within a month, ten thousand copies of *Alphise* had been sold. The authoress's portrait was to be seen in every bookseller's window, and Fashion consecrated this masterpiece by creating *"toilettes à l'Alphise"*, which the beauties of every capital wore for several seasons. "Never," wrote Goethe to one of his friends on October 15, 1779, "has the impartial study of the human heart, in its most secret mechanisms, been taken so far. . . . Such sincerity is alarming, for it is impossible to achieve this degree of knowledge without having suffered oneself the passion so admirably described. What I know of our friend forbids me to entertain such a supposition, but may we not imagine that Iphigénie de Seewiesen, predestined to harvest in later ages the heritage of ancient Greece, recalls the time when she lived among the gods, recognizing no morality but theirs, obeying no other laws but her own?"

This astonishing novel described, in effect, the guilty passion of a father for his daughter, and if *Alphise* won its author the approbation of the literati, it deprived her, on the other hand, of the esteem of the neighbouring society, which was scandalized. Many persons whom the haughty Iphigénie had refused to receive at Weissendorf took their revenge by declaring that her book was a veiled autobiography, and announced everywhere that they were closing the doors of their honest abodes to the chatelaine of Weissendorf. Mademoiselle de Seewiesen, sovereignly indifferent to public opinion, paid no attention whatever to this measure, but her father, in whom all saw the hero of *Alphise*, was overwhelmed by it. His paternal pride was the object of the most dreadful suspicions, and the ostracism to which he found himself subjected deprived him of the company of his oldest friends.

For several years longer life at Weissendorf passed in the fashion which Mademoiselle de Seewiesen had imposed upon her intimates: a kind of slavery from which its victims were liberated only by death. Monsieur de Seewiesen disappeared first, the martyr of a broken heart. His eldest son Ajax, captain of a company of Trabans, fell into the hands of the Turks and was impaled beneath the walls of Constantinople on the occasion of the Sultan's wedding festivities. The second son, Achille, perished at sea during the shipwreck of a vessel bearing him to the New World, where he intended to seek his fortune. Hector, the third son, was roasted alive in the fire that ravaged the Burgtheater in Vienna, and the fourth, Ulysse, blew his brains out in a London gaming house after having lost on his word over three hundred thousand pounds. His sister paid his debts by sacrificing almost her entire fortune. These various catastrophes effected no breach in her impassivity, and she found in them merely the subjects of four tragedies: *The Mortal Stake*, *Shipwreck'd Illusions*, *The Fiery Scene* and *Love Is a Game of Chance*. She had these plays put on by a troupe of amateurs, and the privileged few who were able to attend the performances declared that they had never seen anything so moving. The actors themselves succumbed to their emotions, and some among them wept more than their roles required.

Popular credulity regarded the singular concatenation of circumstances that caused the violent deaths of Mademoiselle de Seewiesen's four brothers as some infernal manoeuvre on the latter's part. She was accused of having cast a spell in order to become sole heir of Weissendorf. In Jena, in Weimar, in Eisenach, reliable persons declared to Count Dietrich von Dittersau, who reports the matter quite faithfully in his journal, that "Mademoiselle de Seewiesen gives herself up to the practice of black magic and summons up the spectres of the early Holy Roman Emperors."

"It is also said that she possesses supernatural powers which are not entirely malignant, since she has produced quasi-miraculous cures. In the village of Kreispach she restored a child seized with convulsions to tranquillity. Peasants say that she drives away the fever by laying her hand on the brows of the afflicted, or by tracing certain cabalistic signs in the air, but this is no doubt exaggerated," comments the Count, who cherished a great desire to meet the sorceress and no doubt wished to reassure himself.

Dietrich von Dittersau was a young Bavarian who was travelling about Europe as much to enrich his frivolous mind as to escape his wife, the daughter of the wealthy banker Johann Sprechartz, of Munich. Their unhappy union had not discouraged his attentions to the fair sex, and he consoled himself by conducting several amorous intrigues at once, notably with the celebrated dancer La Carlona, as well as with the Princess von Slavenitz, who was to remain the *grande passion* of his existence. Of an enthusiastic and consequently rather naïve character, vainglorious and convinced that he was born to accomplish great things, he was a worshipper of great men. He easily disarmed the thunders with which his intrusions were occasionally greeted, winning favour by compliments of a calculated ingenuity, and subsequently maintained an assiduous correspondence with most of them. His imagination had been inflamed by the enumeration of Mademoiselle de Seewiesen's charms and talents, and he was determined to force the doors of Weissendorf. These are the terms by which he relates, in his journal under the date of April 27, 1790, that first visit:

"A courier preceded me, charged to announce my arrival at Weissendorf during the course of Wednesday, but so great was my impatience to find myself face to face with the Divinity"— this is his fashion of referring to Mademoiselle de Seewiesen— "that I travelled without relays and reached the village in the morning, following close upon my messenger's heels. I engaged a room at the inn in order to rest for several hours and make an appropriate toilet before presenting myself at the château, where I wished to appear to my advantage. My luggage included the works of the Divinity, which I had brought along in order to reread them near the very localities where this woman of genius conceived them, but I had no need to consult the texts, for there was not a line I did not know by heart! While contemplating the brown tile roofs of the château, I opened my book at random, closed it, opened it again, incapable of fixing my attention, so great was my anxiety. I was served a light repast in my room, which I accompanied with a bottle of Rhine wine brought along with Mademoiselle de Seewiesen's works in order to give myself courage to confront their authoress. It was not necessary for me to drink, for already the thought that I was less than a quarter of a league away from the most sublime woman who has ever existed plunged me into an exaltation bordering on intoxication. I had requested a stableboy to carry to the château a note in which I sought the favour of being received. From my window, I could see the fellow making for the château with so heavy and laggard a step that I was filled with impatience. When I saw him returning I could contain myself no longer, and rushed out to meet him. The expression on his face was so sullen that I anticipated for a moment a refusal from the Divinity, by which, out of consideration for me, he was so aggrieved; but in a voice as hesitant as his gait he told me: 'Her Ladyship expects you at two o'clock. . . .' Ah! The good-natured boy! Had he not been so coarse, I should have thrown myself on his neck to signalize my delight at such news. I regretted that he was so indifferent to my emotion. How is it possible to live in such proximity to genius without feeling its effects? I hastily finished my meal and then made a short excursion through the countryside in order to calm my excitement. As I walked, I plucked a few flowers to offer to my idol: but I feared lest their modesty cause them to be disdained, and cast them into a brook. The current whirled them about for a few seconds, then swept them away. Even so do we resist a brief while before being swept away in our turn by the river of oblivion which spares no one, alas, and as I took the road to Weissendorf I was musing sadly that perhaps the day would come when no one would recognize the name of Mademoiselle Iphigénie de Seewiesen, who seems nonetheless destined to defy the centuries for all eternity.

"My heart was beating hard when I pulled the bell at the postern gate of the château. A lackey opened it and without a word led me through several empty rooms to a tiny chamber where I was to find the Divinity. She was sitting before a cylindrical desk laden with books and papers. Her back was towards me. I saw at first a mass of hair lightly powdered and dressed without coquetry, then, slowly, her head turned towards the door through which I had just entered and a pair of eyes of admirable lustre were fixed upon me. At that moment I was annihilated by the magnetism of this gaze. All the elegant phrases I had so carefully prepared in order to explain my visit vanished from my memory. That penetrating gaze rendered any pretext futile; my name itself was no more than a pretext. What did it matter that my father was a Chamberlain of the Elector of Bavaria? I fell to my knees.

"'Mademoiselle,' I stammered, beside myself, 'I have come to see you. . . .'

"The platitude of my words made me blush at once, but Mademoiselle de Seewiesen dissipated my embarrassment by requesting me to rise and by inquiring about my journey with a cheerful expression. She told me, smiling, that she was acquainted with the leader of a band of brigands active in the region and offered to give me a safe-conduct in case I should be attacked upon my return. I was astonished to find this great lady, this illustrious authoress, so unconventional. When I told her that I had taken lodgings at the inn of her village, she replied that I had been unkind not to seek from her a hospitality she would have been happy to offer. Knowing how much Mademoiselle de Seewiesen loves solitude and dreads to be disturbed, I judged from these favourable words that I had produced some impression upon her mind. This immediately restored my natural verve. I questioned her respectfully as to her work; I told her of the transports I had experienced upon reading *Alphise* and admitted that my happiness would be great indeed were I allowed to see the manuscript of this sublime work. The latter had remained with the printer, but she showed me several pages on which were noted the ideas developed in her work. I entreated her to give one of them to me as an earnest of our acquaintance, and she consented to do so with a good grace. Upon my further insistence, she agreed to read me several passages of a new drama whose subject she had borrowed from the Italian Renaissance, and then she declared that she had sufficiently satisfied my curiosity, and the conversation took a more general turn. We spoke of her friends, of Councillor von Goethe, whom I had visited during my stay in Weimar, of the poet Wieland, of Frau von Stein, of the Ducal Court and of that of my own country. She expressed herself wittily upon every subject, imparting to her phrases turns of such vivacity that I thought I saw playing before me fountains made iridescent by the sunlight. They sprang up continually from a word, an idea, a glance. . . . Sometimes Mademoiselle de Seewiesen changed her tone. The fountains yielded to the powerful and regular stream of a monologue by which the Divinity explained to me—with what clarity! with what simplicity!—a theory or a conception dear to her heart. I could have remained for hours listening to her, charmed by the beauty of the images, by the music of the words. No contradiction was thinkable. Everything appeared clear, convincing and magnificent.

"We approached the domain of politics. Recent events in France inspired her to observations stamped with the greatest wisdom. She predicted that grave disorders would agitate this kingdom, and that if the sovereigns of the other nations did not take care their repercussion would extend to all of Europe.

" 'The laws of history, like those of the stars, indicate that great upheavals are at hand,' she specified; 'yet order and justice will triumph over chaos and bloodshed.'

"I expressed anxiety at once as to my own fate, but she reassured me with a smile:

" 'You are born under a happy star, and you shall be on the side of the victors. . . .'

"May it please Heaven that, should Mademoiselle de Seewiesen's sinister predictions prove to be exact, the last of them, too, will not fail to be realized!

"In order to dissipate the distress which her remarks had caused me, she volunteered to escort me over her domain, and we left the château, the Enchantress leaning familiarly upon my arm. I marvelled that to the merest details of domestic life she brought the same quality of intelligence as to the loftiest subjects. She was great even in small things, as worthy of respect and admiration in her barnyard as in the most formal of salons. The very animals came to meet her as soon as she drew into sight, and I was struck by this fact, seeing in it a manifestation of that strange power she exerts over beasts and men alike, and of which the peasants speak with a kind of superstitious dread. We advanced, chatting the while, as far as a little Greek temple whose columns were reflected in the clear waters of a pond. Its pediment was silhouetted with startling clarity against the sky which, in this spot, seemed a deeper blue than above the château or the wood. I observed as much to Mademoiselle de Seewiesen. She averred that I was correct.

" 'It is the Orient sky, like myself an exile . . . ,' she murmured.

"Then I told her that I had known the poet Chénier in Paris, and recited some of his verses. She listened to me with passionate attention. When I was done, she launched into an extraordinary improvisation which conjured up before my delighted eyes the Greece of ancient days. By the mere power of the word, she created anew a vanished world, before which the present seemed miraculously to fade away like the shades of night before the fires of the dawn. Mademoiselle de Seewiesen was transfigured. Her splendid throat pulsed with a swifter rhythm, her eyes sparkled, the lustre of her lips and her complexion were heightened by emotion. Her white gown, falling straight to the ground without the slightest ornament, had become a toga that draped her in majesty. She was no longer a woman of our time, beautiful still despite her age, but a goddess incarnate before a thunderstruck mortal. Suddenly the evening wind arose, and a strange music could be heard: a melodious plaint which filled the air now with heartrending accents, now with long, scarcely modulated sighs, gentle and confused as whispers. The plaint died away imperceptibly, then new harmonies resounded closer at hand. This time it was a livelier music, trembling with restrained voluptuousness which after a series of brilliant variations ended on a long trill of amorous ecstasy. I had fallen silent, surprised, disquieted, and at the same time enchanted. Mademoiselle de Seewiesen listened, motionless, to this symphony that seemed to come from another world. The sun was setting behind the little temple, and the Enchantress looked to me now like one of those black-paper silhouettes that are outlined by the lamplight.

" 'It is only the Aeolian harps,' she told me, indicating the strings of these instruments fixed between the columns of the temple.

"I was so troubled by a thousand inexpressible sentiments that I almost believed I saw, in the shadows that were lengthening around us, those of the gods evoked by Mademoiselle de Seewiesen. Was it not their fingers that sounded upon the strings of the Aeolian harps? I felt myself prepared for some supernatural revelation which would crown this unique day, but nothing further was vouchsafed. The wind gradually subsided, the moaning of the harps faded until it was no more than a murmur as discreet as the conversation of lovers, and then they ceased altogether.

"It was almost dark when we returned to the château. A supper was awaiting us on a little table laid in the library. After this repast, whose frugality it pleased her to remark upon as necessary to the proper functioning of the mind, she spoke to me of her family, of the tragic fate of her four brothers, and then questioned me, attempting to provoke my confidences. I had come to hear the Divinity, to harvest her oracular words, and I was reluctant to speak of myself, knowing how readily I would enjoy doing so. She nevertheless insisted that I furnish some account of myself, and I yielded to her desire. I told her of my life, my marriage, and ventured to speak of La Carlona, as well as of the sentiments that attached me to the Princess von Slavenitz. She wonderfully disentangled the double chaos of my existence and my conscience. She gave me, in addition, such wise counsel, such noble encouragement, that I left her moved to tears by her kindness.

"I returned to the village by foot, and on the way I made an encounter that intrigued me greatly. I was walking along, my mind entirely filled with Mademoiselle de Seewiesen, when a stranger passed me in the opposite direction and wished me good night. From his accent I knew it was a man of the region, and I would have attached no importance to this commonplace fact if at that very moment the moon, which clouds had veiled almost entirely, had not suddenly been revealed, illuminating the countenance of this late stroller. Its beauty was such that I was struck dumb with astonishment. I stopped, hesitating to turn around in order to admire once again that marvellous face, then I reflected that I must have been deceived by some play of light and shadow, which had shown me under an un-real aspect a physiognomy no doubt quite ordinary, and I con-tinued on my way to the village without seeing a living soul. It was near midnight, and my valet had fallen asleep while wait-ing for me. What in the world could that handsome stranger have been doing at so late an hour, and on a road which led no-where save to the château? My imagination, given over to the romantic, preferred to interpret the episode as a *rendezvous galant* with the Divinity, but would she condescend to love a simple mortal?"

Summoned by La Carlona to join her in Vienna without de-lay, Count Dietrich von Dittersau had no time to verify this hy-pothesis. He left the following day, but the Divinity had so profoundly bewitched him that he did not fail to make a de-tour through Weissendorf three years later, on his way to take possession of his late father-in-law's estates. He stopped there for several days, and if he did not lodge at the château, he at least spent all his days there. Mademoiselle de Seewiesen held him in particular esteem, which flattered without surprising him, accustomed as he was to affording others pleasure. His journal abounds in picturesque details concerning the chate-laine's private life, and he produces the key to the enigma which his meeting with the handsome stranger had proposed three years before. He recognizes him in the person of "a new footman, handsome as could be, but stupid as well, and for whom the Sorceress seems to have conceived the most singular affection. He does not leave her room, though he is required for no services there"—he writes naïvely enough—"and makes himself unendurable. She addresses a thousand cajol-eries to him and does not attempt to dissimulate the sentiments he inspires in her, which cannot help but appear surprising on the part of so rational a woman. She has shown me several portraits she has executed of him. He has, in truth, an extremely fine head, but such company does not become a woman of quality, and I was distressed to see the divine Iphigénie maintain so familiar an intercourse with a man of his condition."

Count Dietrich then complains that the favourite's presence hampers any conversation, and, vexed and doubtless a trifle jealous, he shortens his stay at Weissendorf. He nevertheless returns to the region the following year, in the month of October 1794, and is indeed alarmed at the lackey-master's growing influence.

"The Sorceress is victim of a baneful enchantment, which has caused her to lose her former serenity," he writes. "She sleeps badly, her eyes are red from weeping. Her complexion is spoilt, her splendid hair has gone grey. The disorder of her *toilette* reveals that of her soul. She abandons coquetry just when the latter is most necessary, and complains of being neglected by a man whom she seeks to retain less by her physical charms than by those of her mind, of which he remains evidently insensible. She writes virtually not at all, leaves her letter unanswered, and is interested in nothing other than this fatal passion, weeping and lamenting all the day, which is indeed sad to see.

"Today, while Karl was out hunting, she could not forbear revealing her heart and making me a number of confidences. She took my hands in hers and tenderly pressed them while calling me her only friend and entreating me not to abandon her in her wretchedness. Even as I mingled my tears with her hers, I could not help evoking the recollection of my first visit to Weissendorf some years earlier, when Mademoiselle de Seewiesen was at the apogee of her reputation, and I judged myself almost unworthy to be received by her. Moved to compassion by such misfortunes following upon such glories, I made her a thousand protestations of my devotion. Encouraged by these assurances, she revealed to me that, in order to be more certain of keeping her lover at her side, she had secretly married him. Although I had already suspected as much, this news afforded me a surprise which I permitted myself to reveal.

" 'How can it be, mademoiselle, that you have so forgotten the elevation of your rank and that of your mind as to unite yourself to a man as deficient in the one as in the other?'

"She replied that she had sufficient intelligence for two, nor had she sought any intellectual commerce in this union, but simply the satisfaction of her mind by that of her senses. The latter, she confessed to me, had always greatly tormented her, despite all appearances to the contrary, and she had yielded to them only by reason of the absolute empire she formerly exercised over Karl. He had long been merely a splendid animal subjected by the desire he felt for his mistress, but the favour he enjoyed had gradually emboldened him. This passion assuaged, he had discovered others—for village girls, for gambling and for brandy. Disappointed in her love, humiliated in her pride, Mademoiselle de Seewiesen, after having been the artisan of her own fall, is now its lucid and, paradoxical as it may appear, its fascinated spectator. In vain I suggested that she abandon Weissendorf and her unworthy spouse in order to withdraw to some tranquil spot where she could live as she chose. In vain did I propose that she leave with me for Vienna, where Princess von Slavenitz would be so happy to receive her. To all the speeches by which I attempted to waken in her a desire for another existence, whether calmer or more brilliant, she opposed a silence by which her refusal could be divined. Her resolution was unwavering.

" 'When one loves,' she told me sadly, 'one loves even to one's own misery. . . .' "

Dietrich von Dittersau was never again to see his fallen Divinity. All correspondence between them ceased, and Mademoiselle de Seewiesen, who had long focused upon herself the attention of the whole of Europe, fell into oblivion. Her death

passed almost unnoticed. A mere handful of gazettes remarked upon the occasion. As she had predicted one spring
evening of the year 1790, grave events overturned the world,
and some twenty-five years later Dietrich von Dittersau found
himself on the side of the victors, indeed seated among them
at the Congress of Vienna. Did he then recall Mademoiselle de
Seeweisen's prophecy and wish to render a last homage by
once more visiting the sites where her strange destiny had been
realized? His journal contains no indication as to the motives
that induced him to make this pilgrimage, and we find there
only the account of his stay in Weissendorf. In the village, he
had been told that since her ladyship's death the château had
been abandoned. The former lackey had left the region, and
no one knew what had become of him. Count Dietrich had his
carriage halt before the gate of the park, and set off to find the
little Grecian temple which had been the witness of one of the
most radiant hours of his youth. It was an October afternoon,
cold and drear. The wind was driving enormous clouds across
the sky. Count Dietrich writes that he walked for a long time
through the wood before finding the temple. Finally he
glimpsed it through the leafless trees. Mademoiselle de Seeweisen had told him one day that it was her wish to be buried
here, and he hoped that this desire had been respected. He discovered a tombstone whose inscription had almost completely
disappeared under a greenish lichen: only the name of Iphigénie was still visible, and he stood staring at it for a long moment, lost in melancholy reflections. Suddenly he thought he
heard a funereal air which tirelessly embellished the same
theme upon three notes. It was a kind of plaint, shriller than
that of the trees bent by the wind, more despairing than that
of a lost soul. Somewhat alarmed, he looked about him, yet
saw no one. Then he recalled a mysterious music heard once
before in this spot. Upon examining the ruins of the temple, he
discovered between the columns several steel wires that vi-

brated with every gust of wind. They were the wreckage of the Aeolian harps Mademoiselle de Seewiesen had installed here in order to capture the music of the gods, and which in her turn she brushed with an invisible hand in order to express the sadness of her disenchanted heart.

On the Thunersee

■ ■ ■ THE GRAND LUNCHEONS that the Prince d'Ancezuno- ■ ■ ■
Terlinden used to give at Schloss Hofenhof, on the shores of
the Thunersee, were generally followed, if time permitted, by
outings in his steam-yacht, a source of the most delicious emotions for the ladies of the party. Their husbands, who claimed
not to have acquired their sea legs, ordinarily declined to accompany them and preferred to remain longer in the Prince's
oriental smoking-room, where they would discuss other men's
wives.

One afternoon in September 1843, on Prince d'Ancezuno's
yacht, several ladies from nearby manors were gliding along,
gracefully lounging against the hand-rail from which they
watched the shores retreat, waving lace kerchiefs in the direction of Hofenhof, whence their delighted husbands echoed
these signals of farewell. It had been decided to venture quite
a distance, as far as Spietz, where Count von Herlach was giving a medieval banquet in the *salle d'armes* of his Schloss. The
weather was magnificent; a light breeze was blowing, which
disordered *toilettes* and made itself the accomplice of a thousand coquetries. On the pretext that the pitching of the boat
upset his balance, the Prince embraced, as though by accident,
the most charming waists and exclaimed over ankles or legs of
which a flutter of skirts vouchsafed him more than a glimpse.

Two ladies, dangerously leaning over the prow, attempted to
plunge the tips of their parasols into the water, while another
took a turn at the helm, uttering cries of delight upon discovering that the boat obeyed her. Leaning against the drum of
one of the wheels, the Baroness von Waldegg requested a

sailor, whose stature she admired, to explain the Compass Rose to her. The Countess von Schoenfels permitted the Prince to persuade her to visit the interior of the yacht, while the Marquise de Feraudaz was reciting stanzas of Lamartine, breathing deeply from her salts bottle the while. It was at this moment that the catastrophe occurred. No one ever knew its precise cause: the families of the victims, the members of the Grand Council and the engineer who had constructed the boiler wasted their days in diverse conjectures or produced contradictory opinions. The only certainty remained the explosion of the boiler and the wreck of the yacht in the middle of the lake. The scattered limbs of a Marquise, three Countesses and several Baronesses, not to mention the widow of a Chevalier of the Holy Roman Empire, were projected into the air before sinking into the deep with the fragments of the machinery. Prince d'Ancezuno and the Countess von Schoenfels, clinging to one another, kept afloat a few moments before vanishing in their turn. There escaped from immediate death only two sailors, who were fished out, terribly burnt, by the Interlaken steamer that had rushed to the vicinity of the disaster. They could give no details concerning this tragedy, which bereaved the aristocracy of the three cantons of Berne, Thun and Fribourg. The days that followed were marked by scenes whose horror long haunted the memories of all who witnessed them. Two magistrates from Berne were seen fighting a duel over a silk-stockinged leg which each of them claimed to have belonged to his wife. The decapitated trunk of the Countess von Worb und Signau was recognized by her lover and offered to the Count, who refused it. The children of Madame de Villargy plied the waters of the lake for three days in the hope of recovering some remains of their beloved mother. The waves cast upon the shore only the Countess de Balterswyl, who was still holding in one hand a fragment of the helm. Her heirs commissioned the sculptor Clésinger to execute a splendid monument which represented her emerging from the waves, her hair loose, her breast bare, one hand clutching the vessel's wheel. After the Sonderbund War, the inscription was obliterated from the pedestal and the Federal Council declared that the statue portrayed "Liberty leading the Destinies of Helvetia". Honest fishermen brought in several hands which the grief-stricken families disputed hotly. On the other hand, two wigs were identified by no one, and were left to the Cantonal Museum of Thun. In the next century, some persons of modest origin claimed them as those of their ancestors. An article in the Bulletin of the Swiss Archaeological Society fortunately meted out justice to these patrician pretentions.

The obsequies of the Prince d'Ancezuno were attended, aside from his family, by only two grateful widowers. The grief of the others afforded the country a fine example of Helvetian fidelity. The Baron de La Poyaz, among others, distinguished himself by a despair all the greater in that his wife was wearing, on the fatal day, the celebrated Barzoi, a diamond which had formerly belonged to Charles the Bold and which one of his ancestors had gleaned upon the battlefield of Morat. The historical origin of this gem and its incomparable yellow tint gave it a considerable value, far above that fixed upon it by the Munich jeweller who had mounted it as a brooch for the baroness. The very evening of the shipwreck, her husband undertook to have the lake dragged at the spot where the ship had foundered, superintending the operations through a spyglass. Beside him, upon the bank, stood his Chaplain, who, assisted by a choirboy, granted absolution to each piece of human debris that was presented to him. Soon only fragments of wood, bits of iron and other such wreckage of no interest to the Baron were being taken from the depths. When all chances of recovering the Barzoi had vanished, he asked the insurance company, with whom he had been prudent enough to register the diamond, to pay him the full amount of the indemnity provided for. The company offered all kinds of difficulties, going so far as to question his good faith, and paid only with the greatest reluctance. It required over ten years, moreover, for the establishment to recover from such a loss.

Monsieur de La Poyaz, however, never recovered at all. The sum of money he received did not restore his jewel, which he regarded as the talisman of his House. It was true that henceforth strange vicissitudes marked the destinies of his entourage. The first was the collapse of the Schürrer Bank, in which the Baron had deposited his entire fortune. He was obliged to sell his Brévillars estate in order to take refuge in a little country house not far from Berne. His elder daughter eloped one day with the village pastor, who was already married. To those who asked him for news of this capricious person, her father replied in a contemptuous tone:

"She is living in Protestantism and in Concubinage!"

And it could be divined that in his eyes the former stage appeared still more indecent than the latter. One of his sons, an officer in the Neapolitan Service, became the lover of the Princess Maria-Pia degli Angeli, whose husband had him assassinated by sbirros in his pay. Another son exchanged the soutane, which he wore quite becomingly, for the diverse costumes of the Biederhaus Theatre in Vienna, whither his mad passion for the diva Mina Floss had led him.

The Baron himself suffered the most humiliating misadventures. He had taken as his second wife one of his own nieces, and this latter, who was half his age, deceived him during summers in the country with a magistrate from the Petty Council, and during winters in Berne with a magistrate from the Grand Council. All these misfortunes had changed his character and profoundly altered his humour. He had fallen into a profound melancholy which rendered him indifferent to the course of existence, spending most of his days in sombre reverie. He was often to be encountered with his clothes in disorder and his steps uncertain, as if he had been drinking. He uttered incoherent words, often stopped to converse with a tree, yet passed his distressed friends without recognizing them. He suffered hallucinations during which he believed he saw the vanished diamond sparkling a few steps before his eyes. At these moments his countenance was transformed. An expression of almost supernatural happiness was painted upon it. Slowly advancing his hand towards the object of his illusion, he apostrophized it in extravagant language and then, upon discovering his error, burst into convulsive sobs. Several times, it had been necessary to lead him to an improvised litter, for his fits were generally followed by a prostration so extreme that he remained senseless wherever he had fallen.

One day, to celebrate his birthday, his wife had the idea of presenting him with a cut-glass replica of the Barzoi. Upon opening the case, the Baron uttered a joyous roar which delighted the hearts of the guests, but no sooner had he taken the diamond in his hand than he perceived the deception, and his wrath was terrible: he hurled the false Barzoi at the Baroness's head and made such ravages among the crockery that the luncheon could not be served. Following this incident, Madame de La Poyaz, fearing, no doubt, to suffer the fate of her porcelain, obtained authorization to have her husband confined in a rest home situated near the Thunersee, not far from Hofenhof, where this tragedy had begun.

The lake air, the tender care of which he was the object, and also the society of persons whose minds were more deranged than his own soon restored the Baron de La Poyaz to some appearance of reason. He was soon enjoying a regime so privileged that he was permitted to wander about the environs at liberty. His principal resort was Schloss Hofenhof, which had reverted, upon the death of Prince d'Ancezuno-Terlinden, to certain Austrian nephews no one had ever seen. A caretaker and his wife aired out the apartments from time to time, but neglected to maintain the park, which in a few years had become a dreadfully wild place. Monsieur de La Poyaz enjoyed wandering there in search of old memories, and the caretakers, who had deep respect for a lordship, even a fallen one, always greeted him with consideration.

One afternoon, when the Baron, according to his custom, was wandering in the park, he happened upon the caretaker's daughter, a girl of some fifteen years. Upon seeing her, he experienced a kind of astonishment: upon her coarse shawl there glittered, like a star fallen from the heavens, the marvellous Barzoi! Monsieur de La Poyaz was struck dumb with surprise and emotion, and then, with a shriek that terrified the girl, rushed upon her in order to wrest away the jewel. The wretched creature, supposing that the old lunatic was about to abuse her favours, uttered shrill cries and attempted to escape, but the Baron seized her by the arm.

"Be still! Be still!" he gasped. "Don't be frightened; I shall do you no harm. . . . I only wish to know who gave you that pretty brooch."

"No one gave it to me," she replied, attempting to free herself. "I found it near the little bridge where there was once a boat. . . ."

And she began to cry. Pressed by the Baron's questions, she recounted that her father had destroyed the wharf where Prince d'Ancezuno's yacht was formerly moored, and one day, when she came to the place to gather firewood, she had discovered the brooch wedged in a lattice.

"And what did your father say, when he saw you wearing this gem?"

The girl's expression grew terrified once more.

"My father does not know I have this brooch. I wear it on my shawl when I am by myself. If he knew, he would surely take it away from me. Oh, monsieur, do not tell him!" she pleaded.

The Baron squeezed her arm a little harder.

"I shall say nothing if you obey me in every particular. First, you must show me the very place where you found this gem. . . ."

The caretaker's daughter dried her tears and docilely led Monsieur de La Poyaz to the shore of the lake, at the place where ten years before a happy company had embarked for eternity. The site was steeped in the melancholy peculiar to abandoned haunts. The pavilion that had lodged the four sailors of the yacht's crew was in ruins; the gaping windows revealed an interior devastated by wind and rain. Of the wharf itself, that had been so graceful with its little roof in the shape of a pagoda, there remained only the pilings, between which the lake's grey water rippled gently. In the distance rose the dark chain of the Bernese Alps, whose summits were lost in the clouds. The girl, parting the reeds that had overgrown the shore, pointed to the first pilings.

"It was here that I found my brooch."

"Where?" the Baron asked, for his attention had been momentarily distracted by recollections of the past.

"Here!" she repeated, and the better to show him the place, she attempted to jump out upon the piling to which she was pointing. She missed her footing, slipped and fell into the lake with a great cry of distress. Monsieur de La Poyaz watched her struggling without understanding the situation, and then a diabolical idea flashed through his darkened mind. He seized a plank forgotten on the bank, but instead of holding it out to the unhappy girl, he used it to keep her head continually beneath the surface of the water. After several moments, she had ceased to stir and remained caught among the reeds. The Baron removed his frock-coat and cautiously lowered himself into the water, which immediately rose to his chest. He had no difficulty drawing the body out of the water. His first concern was to take possession of the Barzoi; next he made certain that his victim showed no further sign of life. Only then did he head for the Schloss, calling for help. His shouts alerted some peasants whose efforts did not succeed, alas, in reviving the girl. The Baron explained that he was walking not far from the place when he had heard heart-rending cries. He had hurried to the spot, but it had been too late to rescue the poor child. The latter's body was carried to her parents, who, despite their grief, found affecting words with which to thank Monsieur the Baron for his courage. The caretaker lent him a suit of clothes and a neighbour harnessed up his *char-à-bancs* to drive him back to the rest home. The news of his exploit won him general approval, followed, a few days later, by his liberation. His wife called for him herself and was astonished at his fine appearance. He complimented her upon her own, which supplied their relationship with just those good graces that had so long been lacking in their conjugal life. Monsieur de La Poyaz saw therein the beneficent influence of the Barzoi, which he carried in his watch fob, in order to be able to look at it at every moment. His happiness, nevertheless, proved to be curtailed in so far as he was obliged to keep the Barzoi concealed. He would have preferred to manifest his delight and show the diamond in broad daylight, even wear it on occasion, whereas he was forced to maintain the secret of his possession. There were few chances that anyone might establish a connection between the discovery of the Barzoi and the drowning of the caretaker's daughter, since no one had seen the gem in the latter's hands, but the insurance company, which, ten years before, had paid out the counter-value of the Barzoi, would not fail to demand its restitution were it ever to learn that the gem had been recovered. The failure of the Schürrer Bank, the consequences of the Sonderbund War and the poor management of the small fortune that remained to him rendered the Baron incapable of reimbursing even a quarter of the sum he had received. Consequently he would have to resign himself to keeping the Barzoi in his pocket; but not content with pressing it in his hand, he could not resist the pleasure of contemplating it, and this occasioned the most singular behaviour imaginable. He was frequently seen to leave the room quite furtively, or else, during a promenade, to turn aside from whatever society he was with in order to take sudden refuge in a bush. Often, during a repast, he ducked under the table as though to caress some pet or to pinch the leg of his dinner partner, but he had no such gallant thoughts and indeed reserved all his amorous glances for his diamond.

The uneasiness of his mind was to be read so clearly upon his face that the Baroness was inspired with alarm, and spoke once again of the rest home on the shores of the Thunersee. Monsieur de La Poyaz hesitated no longer: to deliver himself from this obsession which would keep him from ending his days in peace, he resolved to sacrifice the Barzoi. One morning, on the pretext of visiting a friend, he took the train for Thun and, once there, embarked upon the Interlaken steamer. It was a September day as calm and harmonious as the one which had formerly unleashed all his misfortunes upon him. The steamer's paddle-wheel regularly plunged into the green and grey water, which splashed up in white sheaves along the drums. The tall, slender, slightly inclined smokestack traced fugitive arabesques upon the blue screen of the sky. Suddenly the Baron, lost in contemplation of flight of gulls above the boat, heard someone speak to him. He turned around and saw a lady, a stranger to him, whose voluminous crinoline indicated a person of condition. She pointed out on the port side a Schloss of romantic aspect, and asked him if he knew its name. He recognized Hofenhof and recalled that he had boarded this boat only to cast into the water, at the very place where Prince d'Ancezuno's yacht had foundered, the diamond which the whole world believed to be at the bottom of the lake. He pulled it feverishly from his pocket, and at that moment a sunbeam caused it to sparkle with a thousand yellow fires, like a second sun. The stranger uttered an exclamation of astonishment. The Baron, bewildered, made a mistake. Instead of hurling the Barzoi overboard, he let it drop upon the deck, at the feet of the elegant lady, and threw himself into the lake.

The Apparitions of Kirmünster

■ ■ ■ FOUNDED IN THE THIRTEENTH CENTURY by Mathilde ■ ■ ■ de Zaerhingen, who came there to be brought to bed in secret, the Convent of Kirmünster owed its fame to August III of Moravia, known as August the Virtuous, for in his fiftieth year, renouncing all pleasures of the senses, he had had his mistress, the beautiful and affecting Aurore de Graffenstatt, confined there. So that this example might be followed by the dignitaries of his Court, he had sent their mistresses to join his own, and it was in consequence that, at the end of the eighteenth century, Kirmünster could boast of having the prettiest nuns of the entire Holy Roman Empire. The monks of Saint-Florentin, a monastery situated on the other side of the high-road, could no longer keep to their beds and had lost no time digging an underground passageway which led them to the objects of their desires. The matter, at first, made little noise in the world at large, and the two establishments would have long continued to offend the sight of the Lord, had the King not intervened and restored order.

One day when, according to his custom, he had arrived un-expectedly in order to visit Reverend Mother Aurore, whose spiritual progress it pleased him to superintend, he had found the latter supping quite gaily with a young novice from Saint-Florentin. The frivolity of their remarks was equalled only by that of their costumes. August the Virtuous immediately had them arrested by the soldiers of his escort, and in order to measure the extent of this scandal he insisted upon visiting the other cells of the Convent. Everywhere he discovered shocking evidences of fornication. If he had formerly attributed the excessive plumpness of certain nuns to the happy effects of a calm and well-ordered life, he realized his error upon penetrating the hall of the chapter-house: half a dozen infants were playing knucklebones with the sacred remains of Mathilde de Zaerhinger, whom a Pope of her family had beatified.

The Monarch's wrath was terrible. The Reverend Mother Superior left for Rome in a cage of iron and ended her days in the Castel Sant' Angelo. The other guilty creatures were arraigned by an ecclesiastical commission, which renewed the rigours of the Inquisition. The monks found themselves condemned to hard labour in the mines of Bohemia; their wretched accomplices were branded with red-hot irons and flogged so cruelly that certain of their number departed this life under the blows. Those who survived, dispersed in several convents, expiated their aberrations by the observance of a discipline so terrible that they envied the lot of their sisters and regretted that they themselves were not dead. Only the fruits of so many sins were spared. Yet the King was determined to prevent them from committing, in their turn, the crimes to which they owed their own lives, and therefore made the male children into choirboys of the Sistine Chapel, and the girls into modest sisters-in-attendance at the turnboxes of various convents. The Monastery of Saint-Florentin was sold to the Order of the Knights of Malta, which established a commandery there. The Convent of Kirmünster, on the other hand, found no purchaser and was ravaged by several mysterious fires whose causes it was never possible to ascertain.

The people of the region reported that the ghosts of the lovely victims still wandered down the corridors and waved torches at the windows, and that by night bloody spots glowed on the stones with a phosphorescent lustre. In the course of the years the Convent had become a kind of romantic ruin, surrounded by obscure legends, and passers-by regarded it in terror, without daring to approach. The lands within its dependency were abandoned, for it was claimed that the springs were poisoned and that the grass killed off the cattle which grazed there. The woods served as a refuge for a number of brigands whose exploits merely augmented the sinister reputation of the place. The Steward of the Crown Domains was therefore quite surprised when, one day of the year 1865, more than fifty years after the death of August the Virtuous, a foreigner presented himself, announcing his intention of buying the Convent of Kirmünster. This person was a wealthy Englishman whom a curious form of melancholy had hitherto condemned to perpetual wanderings. On board a steam-yacht, he had crossed all the seas of the globe, and it was rumoured that he owed a share of his wealth to the slave trade. Now he was crossing Europe in a special car which he arranged to have attached to the regular trains. He informed the Steward that he was weary of travelling and hoped, henceforth, to enjoy some repose in an agreeable site. That of Kirmünster, glimpsed from the window of his train carriage, had delighted him, and, despite its unfortunate celebrity, the Englishman was resolved to live there.

"The ghosts will not frighten you, Milord?" the Steward inquired.

"I spent my childhood in a Scottish castle where a Queen had been poisoned, an Archbishop assassinated, and where my great-grandfather hanged himself upon learning of the defeat of Prince Charles Edward. . . ." Lord Ruthermore of Glencoe contented himself with replying.

For the sum of fifty thousand florins he became the seigneur of Kirmünster and undertook to make vast renovations and repairs there which constituted the amazement of the peasants of the region. The Convent itself was entirely restored and surmounted by an octagonal tower whose construction provoked much comment. A giant telescope was installed upon the summit, and Lord Ruthermore thereby gained a reputation as an astronomer, which distinction was confirmed by several interesting communications to the Royal Academy of Geography. The neighbourhood soon grew accustomed to his eccentricities, to his Hindu servants, to his steam-carriage that staved in so many bridges, and it was only regretted that his eremitic humour kept him sequestered from the life of Society, the company of the phantoms apparently proving sufficient for him. Upon his arrival in the country, he had shown a certain curiosity about the legends which concerned his residence, and had caused some research to be carried out in the archives of Budéjovice in order to disinter there the history of Kirmünster; thereafter he had by degrees immured himself in a lofty solitude which no visitor dared disturb. Kirmünster and its chatelain would have drawn no further attention to themselves if certain strange events had not occurred which excited first the curiosity and then the consternation of the entire province.

The first of these was the conversion of the Count de Bresen, who claimed to have seen his grandmother, one of the companions of Aurore de Graffenstatt, wandering upon the road between the two religious houses. He had never known her in life, but numerous portraits kept the memory of her beauty alive in his ancestral château. He had identified her all the more easily in that she was wearing a panniered dress in every detail similar to that which had inspired Liotard to paint her as the *"Jolie Parfumeuse"*. This vision unsettled his mind: he broke with his mistress, recalled his wife and henceforth led a most edifying life, filled with fasts and other mortifications of the flesh. Since the Count de Bresen had always passed for a little mad, no one attached much importance to this affair, but several months later people were obliged to admit that it was not so devoid of foundation as had been supposed.

As it happened, the ghost of Aurore de Graffenstatt appeared in the same place to the horrified eyes of Prince Heinrich von Kanzelhöhe, her grandnephew and governor of the neighbouring city. His horses bolted and precipitated his berlin into a ditch, which did not fail to add to his consternation. While his equipage was being dragged out of the mire, the

Prince asked asylum from the Commander of Saint-Florentin, who showed a certain scepticism upon hearing his story. The Prince had no sooner left, however, than on the following night a marvellous creature was seen floating in midair a few steps from the Commander, who took it for the Holy Virgin and immediately fell to his knees. The description he gave of this pious vision permitted the Curator of the Royal Museum of Painting to affirm that the figure in question was that of Constance de Steinbrugg as she had been portrayed by Lampi. A dispute arose between the Curator and the Commander, who had already indited a *mémoire* upon this manifestation of Divine Grace of which he had been the object.

Three weeks later it was Barbe de Heidenlandt, her throat and shoulders shamelessly displayed, a perverse smile upon her lips, who appeared to her own daughter on her way to the capital, where she was to attend the baptism of her twenty-eighth grandson. She was old and infirm; the shock of her emotion hastened her end. She expired in the Commander's arms, entreating him to veil the maternal nudity.

Hedwige de Chokowitz, who was known as "*la belle Polo-naise*" at the period when she constituted the delight of Marshal Bürkli, the friend of August the Virtuous, one night stopped the Budéjovice diligence, whose exhausted team no longer had the strength to take the bit in its teeth. Highway robbers who happened to be passing in the vicinity seized this occasion to pillage the terrified travellers. This last event roused public opinion to such a pitch that King Otho IV ordered an investigation to be held. The Minister of Police, the Bishop's Coadjutor and the Royal Librarian were dispatched to Kirmünster, charged to study the phenomenon, discover its causes and reassure, by their presence, the populace which superstitious fear was beginning to demoralize. They remained a month at the Commandery, without a single ghost deigning to manifest itself. Wearied by this futile vigilance, they relaxed their supervision and accepted several invitations to the neighbouring châteaux. One evening, as the three of them were returning from a dinner with Lord Ruthermore, whom these tales of revenants seemed to amuse enormously, they saw silhouetted against the Commandery wall several figures in sackcloth. They vanished when the representatives of the Crown, mastering their alarm, attempted to approach them. Since the investigators had been drinking Porto quite copiously, they dared not recount this vision, which may have been only the product of their imaginations. They returned crestfallen and empty-handed to the Court, where the King accorded them a glacial reception. His dissatisfaction was increased when the governor informed him that immediately after the departure of the illustrious investigators the ghosts had resumed their infernal sarabands.

Agathe Heilmühl, whose liaison with the Crown Prince had once made her famous, appeared virtually naked to a young shepherd, who had thereby contracted a malign fever. His dog had gone mad and bitten half the flock.

The following day, at the same hour, and once again in front of the Commandery, Aurore de Graffenstatt had slowly passed on the arm of August the Virtuous, followed by a train of several ladies of the court whose names had been immortalized by the scandalous chronicles of the period. The Knights of Malta, whom this event had roused from their beds, crowded to the highroad in order to contemplate this alluring procession, a veritable challenge to their vows of chastity. When Barbe de Heidenlandt released the diaphanous veils that enveloped her person, one of the Knights rushed towards her, his arms outstretched to enjoy that felicity which she appeared to offer, but no sooner had he taken a few steps than this mirage vanished and the Commandery found itself suddenly plunged into utter darkness. The Knights of the Order returned to their cells, agitated by the same sentiments as those formerly endured by their predecessors, the monks of Saint-Florentin. Alas, they had no opportunity of succumbing to the same temptations!

From that night on, the apparitions became so frequent that it was possible to predict and observe them as though they had been a public spectacle. Relatives of the lovely victims acquired the habit of visiting Saint-Florentin, one in order to see an ancestress, others a mother or grandmother whose features had charmed their childhoods or haunted their dreams. The Baron von Gschwinder sent to Vienna for a photographic apparatus in order to capture the likeness of his grandmother, the celebrated Hedwige de Chokowitz, whose biography he was writing. He obtained from this attempt a portrait so remarkable that the King himself decided to visit Kirmünster in order to contemplate these curious manifestations from the Beyond. Since the former Monastery of Saint-Florentin was not large enough, nor sufficiently comfortable, to receive the Sovereign, the latter accepted the hospitality Lord Ruthermore offered him. Otho IV and his retinue arrived at Kirmünster late one July afternoon in the year 1866. Their host came to meet them in his sumptuous steam-carriage which spread terror among the carriage horses of the Court. As he passed before the Commandery, the King could see the grandstand that had been erected along the highroad, opposite the wall before which the spirits were accustomed to stroll up and down.

"How does it happen that these ghosts especially favour this holy place, and do not prefer to it your own residence, which formerly belonged to them?"

Lord Ruthermore smiled wryly.

"I have so evil a reputation, Sire, that even phantoms flee my company. . . . Perhaps they are attempting to enter the Commandery in order to do penance there!"

Towards eleven in the evening the Sovereign and his entourage left the hall where Lord Ruthermore had offered them a magnificent banquet; and after taking a short walk through gardens illuminated by hundreds of toches, they reached the grandstand set up before the Commandery. In the neighbouring fields were encamped, more or less comfortably, all the nobility of the region, who had hastened to the spot in order to

see at one and the same time their King and the strange phenomena which had motivated his August Presence. A great
tumult marked the arrival of the Court; everyone struggled to
take a place as close to the Sovereign as possible. Lords of importance, refusing to go on foot among this multitude, had
their vehicles driven forward as far as the grandstand, and remained in their carriages in order to observe the spectacle:
people were knocked down by the horses, whiplashes fell upon
anonymous shoulders. This disorder gradually abated, and towards midnight an anxious silence reigned over a crowd esti-
mated at over five thousand persons. The torches had been extinguished, the carriage lamps blown out. Only the windows
of Kirmünster gleamed through the darkness, for Lord Ruthermore, declining the King's invitation, had preferred to remain at home.

The last strokes of midnight were echoing through the air,
when a lively glow illuminated the wall of the Commandery
and a legendary silhouette was outlined there, readily recog-
nizable, since it was that of the Emperor Napoleon. Another
joined it, whom most of the observers recognized as that of the
unfortunate Duke of Enghien. Murmurs rose on all sides. The
French Ambassador stirred in his armchair and made as if to
withdraw, but had no opportunity to do so. Dantesque visions
nailed all the spectators to the spot. Hell opened its jaws before
them and, amid the flames, they could discern August the Virtuous surrounded by loathsome reptiles whose heads pierced a
curtain of russet vapours. The King paled with fear; ladies
fainted without anyone daring to bring them succour; others
fell to their knees and began to pray aloud. The boldest of
those present would have given ten years of their lives to be a
hundred leagues from the place, but it was not possible to leave
before the King. Suddenly someone stood up and ran towards
the thick of the flames. A cry of anguish greeted this folly.
Everyone recognized the Baron von Gschwinder; it was believed that he had lost his reason. Two of his friends attempted

to save him, but before they had reached him an enormous laugh was heard and all saw the Baron strolling among the serpents with the serenity of the Prophet Daniel in the furnace. Several times over he stretched out his hand to touch the wall of the Commandery, then he turned about, looked up into the sky, and returned towards the grandstand where Otho IV, confounded by this new prodigy, no longer knew which Saint to invoke. The Baron's face was more delighted than alarmed.

"Fear nothing, Your Majesty," he said; "there is no diabolic sorcery in these manifestations. It is only an imposture. . . ."

He pointed to the tower of Kirmünster.

"Lord Ruthermore has played a trick upon us, in his fashion. He has installed on the summit of his residence some kind of magic lantern of gigantic proportions. It must be equipped with a mechanism which permits the images to succeed one another with such rapidity that the illusion of movement is created, but it is only an illusion and there is no danger, as Your Majesty can discover for himself."

The King hesitated, then let himself be convinced by the Baron to follow him. Both of them had no sooner taken a few steps than the vision suddenly disappeared. When their eyes once again grew accustomed to the darkness, they saw nothing more than the wall of the Monastery of Saint-Florentin, of sepulchral pallor. Clouds veiled the moon's face. Already the rumour that the wonder had been a fraud was running through the ranks of the spectators, whose voices began to sound a little more animated, when a blinding flash cleft the heavens, followed by a thunderous explosion that cast everyone to the ground. Great blocks of stone and iron girders whistled over their heads and landed some hundred yards from the grandstand, crushing several sentries who had been posted there to prevent the phantoms from approaching, if such had been their fancy. After a few seconds, which seemed centuries, a flame leaped up in the direction of Kirmünster and, from the brilliance of the blaze, it was seen that the octagonal tower had collapsed. Every effort exerted by the local peasantry could not control the fire, which left only ruins. Lord Ruthermore's body was never found, and no one could discover whether, seeing his trickery unmasked by the Baron von Gschwinder, he had blown himself up, or whether a defect in the mysterious mechanism had provoked its explosion. Among the wreckage, only a piece of clockwork was recovered whose contrivance appeared sufficiently curious for the Baron von Gschwinder to see in it a confirmation of his hypothesis. He also gathered from the debris certain fragments of glass, admirably painted, whose piecing together permitted the face of Aurore de Graffenstatt to be reconstructed. After his death, the machinery, the slivers of glass and one lens still intact were bequeathed to the Royal Conservatory of Budéjovice. They can still be seen there, in a glass case, with this caption: "Debris from the first cinematograph, called the 'Kirmünster Projector', invented by Lord Ruthermore of Glencoe."

"Die Fledermaus"

■ ■ ■ VIENNA WAS THE FIRST STOP on the wedding journey ■ ■ ■
of Conrad de Murten, Lieutenant in the Fifty-ninth Regiment
of Archduke Rainer, and his bride. They planned to remain in
the city only a few days, in order to see its principal curiosities,
before visiting Graz to call on some cousins, and thence to
Venice, where the Lieutenant had engaged for a month a floor
of the Palazzo Morosini. The eve of their departure for Graz
was to be spent, the Murtens decided, at the theatre, and they
asked the *maître d'hôtel* to suggest an amusing play.

"I should prefer a comedy with some music in it. . . ." Madame de Murten specified.

Her grandmother had once taken as a lover the Kapellmeis-
ter of Prince von Mecklemburg-Strelitz, and she had been
brought up by the old lady as a worshipper in the cult of melody. The *maître d'hôtel* advised them to hear *Die Fledermaus*,
the latest operetta by Johann Strauss the younger. All Vienna
was talking about it, and it was the greatest success of the sea-
son. He offered to obtain seats for them and managed to find a
pair in a stage box. The young Baroness de Murten, who had
never seen any theatrical performances save those of amateurs
in neighbouring châteaux, was dazzled by the magnificence of
the hall, the brilliance of the crystal chandeliers and the elegance of the gowns. She expressed an almost childish joy at
every detail that affected her husband agreeably. He himself
enjoyed only military music and regarded all other kinds as a
frivolous pastime which he habitually disdained, but he had
just heard someone say that the Archdukes would attend the
theatre that evening, and at these words his face lit up. His eyes

fixed on the Imperial Box, he was eagerly awaiting Their Highnesses' arrival, delighted by this occasion to manifest his devotion to the Dynasty.

The first bars of the overture greeted the appearance of the Archdukes, whose breasts gleamed with the jewels of many hereditary orders. Conrad de Murten was absorbed in their contemplation while his wife fell into a kind of voluptuous ecstasy; her elbows on the edge of the box, her lorgnette in her hand, she followed the actors without losing a gesture of their impersonations. Nostrils quivering, her mouth half open, she appeared to drink in the delicious music that acted upon her like a philtre. Her expression was indeed so singular that the Baron, torn from his admiration of the Dynasty, was intrigued by it. Hitherto he had seen this expression upon his wife's face only in the course of the amorous tourneys that had made their nights at the hotel so illustrious. For an instant, the notion that she had been aroused by a spectator or a musician occurred to him. He leaned forward over her shoulder to look down into the house. He glimpsed no face that seemed to him worthy of holding his attention, and smiled, reassured. Agathe was so young, so enthusiastic! She was merely enjoying herself. . . . It was her first evening at the theatre, and he was reluctant to diminish her pleasure by reproaching her for showing it in so naïve a manner.

Madame de Murten followed the developments of the second act with an even more impassioned interest. She tapped her left foot in time to the music, followed the conductor's movements with her fan, nodded her head, and seemed in general subject to the liveliest emotion. Her breast heaved with an accelerated rhythm, and long, deep sighs of satisfaction occasionally escaped from her throat as though she were gasping for breath, and in his heart of hearts the Baron congratulated himself upon having wed so ardent a creature. Once the curtain had fallen upon the last act and the applause had ceased, Madame de Murten rose to her feet with somnambulistic rigidity, her eyes blank, and mechanically followed her husband out of the theatre. In the fiacre that drove them back to the hotel she took some time to regain her spirits, indifferent to the Baron's exclamations at the Court equipages, but no sooner had she reached their rooms than she manifested a sudden gaiety and began to hum the tunes she had heard. She stopped only at dawn, when she fell asleep at last, crushed with fatigue. Monsieur de Murten did not offer any complaint about this little concert, for in another domain his bride had that night given evidence of a virtuosity so astonishing that he remembered it all the rest of his life. Later, indeed, when he had reached middle age and was obliged to resort to artifices to revive a faltering passion, he always asked his mistress to sing him a refrain from *Die Fledermaus*, which never failed to rouse him at the supreme moment. As a matter of fact, that was how he died, in the middle of a roundelay.

Agathe de Murten wakened at nearly ten; she seemed to have recovered her habitual state. Her husband was about to have their luggage removed when she implored him, clasping her arms around his neck, to postpone their departure for another day so that she might return to the theatre. The Baron let himself be entreated a while to enjoy the pleasure of this embrace, then he yielded good-naturedly enough, stipulating a single proviso that kept them in bed until it was time for lunch. That afternoon they went to the Prater for ices and in the evening found themselves in the same seats as the night before. The Archdukes, on this occasion, did not attend the spectacle, and Monsieur de Murten cast a nostalgic glance at the empty box. Contrary to his fears, he was not bored for an instant, for at the first notes of the music his wife was seized by an exaltation so delightful to behold that he followed the progress of the entire play upon her face. He even applauded with all his heart, realizing that the night to come would recompense him for his indulgence. And indeed, when they had regained their rooms at the hotel, Madame de Murten abandoned herself to the joys of the marriage bed with an ardour even exceeding that of the night before.

The young couple awakened quite late in the morning, and since the hour for the train to Graz had already passed, the Baron consented to postpone their departure for another day. They spent the afternoon visiting various churches and then, before dinner, Madame de Murten went upstairs to dress. Upon seeing her attired in an evening gown, her husband asked her if she intended to go to a ball.

"No, my dear," she said with a slightly embarrassed laugh, "not to a ball but to the theatre!"

"To the theatre! What theatre?"

"Why, the one we went to last night! The operetta is so wonderful that I shall never tire of hearing it."

The Baron's countenance grew stern.

"No, my dear, don't be angry with me! I've arranged everything with the porter, and he's taken two seats for us. Would you refuse this pleasure to your little wife who loves you so?"

And with these words she put her arms on her husband's shoulders, and offered her lips to the moustaches that were bristling with irritation. The Baron did not resist this engaging invitation, and the Baroness was obliged to dress her hair all over again before going downstairs to dinner.

This third performance of *Die Fledermaus* produced upon Madame de Murten an effect still more extraordinary than the first two. She astonished the house by the *bizarrerie* of her behavior, laughing or crying at the oddest moments and attracting all eyes by the irregularity of her gestures. The Baron nearly died of shame and congratulated himself upon the fact that the Archdukes were not there. He made several attempts to calm his wife, none of which produced the slightest effect. Their return to the hotel was a veritable scandal: his wife sang various refrains from the operetta at the top of her lungs and kept time to them with such an agitation of her whole body that she communicated an identical movement to the carriage. Passers-by who encountered this vehicle must have supposed it to be carrying some drunkard to his residence, and they were not so very far from the truth, for Madame de Murten had just experienced an intoxication which was never to subside. Under the porter's sardonic eye, the couple returned to their rooms, animated by various sentiments. The night happily provided a remedy for this situation, and the Baroness took advantage of the new victory she granted her husband in order to persuade him to remain in Vienna one day more.

A day, for her, was an evening she might spend at the theatre in order to see once again the incomparable *Fledermaus*. After having refused to accompany her, the Baron decided to attend the performance after all, fearing lest in his absence his wife might cause a more considerable scandal. His fears were entirely warranted, for Madame de Murten conducted herself, as soon as the curtain had risen, in such a strange fashion that the house physician presented himself and diagnosed her condition as a *crise de nerfs*. The Baroness was carried to the Green Room and, once there, was laid upon a sofa. During the intermission, Johann Strauss, informed that a lady of quality had been taken ill, came to pay his respects. Madame de Murten received him with such transports of joy as to arouse the Baron's jealousy.

"Ah! Maestro!" she exclaimed. "Come and restore the damage that your bewitching music has wrought! It will drive me mad, and I cannot do without it!"

Flattered, Johann Strauss bowed and was about to kiss her hand, when Madame de Murten, with a sudden impulse, threw herself upon his neck, saying:

"Grant me the accolade of genius!"

Monsieur de Murten did not at all appreciate this manifestation of genius and attempted to take his wife home before the second act began. She offered a sudden and savage resistance.

"If you wish to go home, I shall not prevent you, but I intend to stay!"

And as the intermission bell was ringing she stood up, gra-

ciously tendered the physician her thanks and made for her
box in a resolute manner. Lieutenant Conrad, choking with
rage inside his uniform, followed her there. The music assuaged his wife's mood, and a few moments after this incredible scene, the first of its kind in their conjugal life, she was
laughing heartily. Her deportment, alas, was quite as eccentric
during the remainder of the entertainment. No one save herself paid any attention to the stage, and the entire audience had
eyes only for the singular performance she was giving in her
box. Monsieur de Murten returned to the hotel convinced that
so extraordinary a passion for music would make his wife famous, but firmly resolved not to share in this celebrity. The
following morning, refusing to hear any argument, he sent
down their luggage and ordered a carriage to drive them to the
station. The coachman waited for some time in front of the
door, and finally took away a Polish lady somewhat the worse
for drink whom the hotel footman deposited almost roughly
upon his cushions. The Baroness Agathe absolutely refused to
leave Vienna, though her husband threatened to abandon her
if she persisted in her obstinacy. An impecunious officer, it
would cost him, in the literal sense of the word, a great deal to
be separated from his wife with whom, moreover, he was still
deeply in love, but he had a sense of dignity and intended to
lead a seemly life, without permitting the caprices of a crazed
melomaniac to disrupt its course.

That evening, when Madame de Murten began to dress for
the theatre, he wished her a cool good night and went to the
library to smoke a cigar, convinced she would not dare attend
the theatre unaccompanied. She did so, however, and her entrance produced a livelier reaction than that of the Princess
Royal of Saxony. Several journalists came to her box to request
interviews. She astonished them by the vivacity of her spirit
and the extravagance of her replies, but since she possessed to
the highest degree that power of seduction peculiar to the
Hungarian nation, she scored a considerable success among

them which was echoed by the gazettes the following day. Upon her return to the hotel, Madame de Murten found a letter from her husband informing her that he had left for Graz, where a family council would shortly convene in order to reach a decision as to her fate. She tore up the letter with a laugh and declared to her chambermaid that henceforth there was nothing to prevent her from going to the theatre every night.

As she did. In less than a week the whole of Vienna had heard this strange story and had fallen in love with its heroine. There were few who sympathized with Lieutenant Conrad de Murten, that coarse creature who did not understand how one could sacrifice everything to the pleasure of hearing music as admirable as that of Johann Strauss. The young woman's presence at each of the performances was one of the principal factors in the extraordinary success this operetta enjoyed, and its composer, delighted to have inspired such a passion, acquired the habit of coming to her box for a chat during the intermissions.

Madame de Murten left the hotel and rented, in the Molkerbastei, a little house dating from Empress Josephine's day in which she established her ménage. Her days were spent playing music in a salon furnished with lyre-back chairs or, if the weather was fine, in the garden, beside an aviary filled with birds of which several, which were mechanical, taught the rest to warble tunes by Strauss. It was here that a delegate from the family council found her when he attempted to restore her to reason; she refused to receive him, merely ordering her attorney to draw up a paper which accorded the Baron de Murten the usufruct of half of her income. Having thereby purchased her liberty, she could now live as she wished, and in several months became one of the most popular figures in Vienna. People crowded to the theatre to get a glimpse of her, and the receipts amounted to a fabulous sum. Never had a work held the boards so long, and it would have exceeded the five-hundredth performance if certain jealous confrères had not intevened with the Royal Superintendant of Theatres in order to have it withdrawn. Consequently the last evening's presentation was announced. When she learned the news, Madame de Murten went to see the director and remained over an hour in his office. Which did not fail to intrigue a number of persons, who, supposing that she had planned some magnificent celebration following the closing performance, decided to attend this latter. The same idea must have occurred to most of the Viennese, for all the seats were already taken, and it was impossible to procure even an inch of standing room.

On the appointed day an enormous crowd thronged all the approaches to the theatre in order to observe the arrival of the privileged spectators, and particularly that of the celebrated Baroness. Their expectation seemed about to be disappointed, for no one appeared, although curtain time was imminent. Rumours circulated: it was said that the performance had been banned on the Emperor's orders. Some clained that Strauss had just had an attack; others declared that he had committed suicide in a lavatory of the Hotel Sacher. The maestro's appearance reassured them. It was followed, some moments later, by that of the Baroness, whose carriage appeared in the square drawn by two white mules, trotting as fast as they could. The crowd fell back to open a passage for it, and when the blackamoor who sat beside the coachman had unfolded the footboard, it burst into frenzied applause that made the team of mules rear. The Baroness, in a magnificent gown, the ostrich feathers in her hair confined by a ruby clasp, was projected by the jolt into the arms of her admirers, who bore her in triumph through an entirely empty house to her box: she had engaged every seat, from those in the orchestra to the highest galleries where the students ordinarily stood. Nothing disturbed the delicious spectacle: eighty actors and actresses performed for a single spectator who experienced on that evening an ecstasy analogous to that of King Ludwig II at the first performance of *Tannhaüser*.

The next day, the Baroness Agathe passed from eccentricity to madness. It was a Sunday, and in Saint Stephen's Cathedral the Cardinal-Primate was celebrating a Pontifical High Mass when, in the middle of the Elevation, a shaky voice struck up the verses of Prince Orlansky. The reaction was considerable: the Cardinal-Primate was so startled that he swallowed all the wine in the chalice and the organist lost his place. Two Swiss Guards attempted to lay hands on Madame de Murten's person, but with a surprising agility she escaped them and began to run down the nave, her arms spread wide as if she were about to take wing, crying: *"Ich bin die Fledermaus!"* A dozen choirboys, spurred on by several archdeacons, set off in pursuit and cornered her in the Savoy Chapel, where, entrenched behind the tomb of Prince Eugene, she sustained a siege worthy of that great captain. She was ultimately forced to capitulate and was carried out by the two Swiss who thundered their halberds victoriously. Restored to her house and sequestered from the public eye, she underwent examination by Doctor Feuerklugg, the celebrated alienist, who declared that he could unfortunately do nothing to ameliorate her condition. He added that, for the moment, the care of a midwife seemed preferable to his own. The Baroness was indeed pregnant and several months later gave birth.

She gave birth to a bat. Not to a real bat, which would immediately have fluttered around her bedchamber, bumping into the walls, but to a kind of tiny hairy monster with deformed limbs. Its arms were united to its body by a membrane; the gigantic ears, the already long and pointed nose, the dark, ashen colour of the skin—everything accentuated the hideous resemblance. The physician confessed he had never seen such a phenomenon, and a nurse who was to be married the following week broke off her engagement, terrified by the unfore-

seen consequences of a *surprise amoureuse*. The only person
who showed any rapture was Madame de Murten. She set
about caring for the little creature so tenderly that, despite her
madness, her attendants decided to leave it with her, perhaps
on the assumption that nothing worse could happen to her. It
was baptized Louise-Victoria-Elizabeth, in honour of the Sovereigns of Baden, of Prussia and of Austria, and Johann
Strauss, filled with remorse, agreed to be its godfather.

The Canoness Vanishes

■ ■ ■ AFTER HER HUSBAND'S DEATH, the wife of a Jewish ■ ■ ■
banker of Vienna became a convert to Catholicism and ordered to be built, upon the shores of the Traunsee, a Gothic
villa whose appearance deceived those pious individuals who
mistook it for a church. Some years later she married once
again, this time another banker, also a Jew, who obliged her to
reassume the religion of her forefathers. She parted company
with the villa, whose architecture reminded her of an unfortunate period in her life, and, as a farewell present to the Roman Catholic Church, presented the structure to the Society of
the Widows and Daughters of the Heroes of Sadowa. This latter institution, uncertain what use to make of its new possession, resolved at last to offer it as a lottery prize. It thus fell to
one Sophie von Winckelried, a half-mad old maid who was
known as the Canoness von Winckelried because she had once
belonged to a Bavarian chapter-house to which only young ladies of ancient lineage were admitted.

Hitherto she had virtually never left the little town of Ei-
senstadt, where she subsisted upon an allowance from her elder brother, the Coadjutor of the Cardinal-Primate of Vienna.
To take possession of her prize was a great event for her. When
the captain of the steamyacht that plied the Traunsee pointed
out the bell-tower of her villa, towering over a clump of trees,
she clapped her hands and wept for joy, to the great astonishment of the other passengers. Upon disembarking, transported by enthusiasm, she missed her footing and fell into the
lake. This misadventure failed to disconcert her in the slightest. Reluctant to waste the minutes necessary to change her

clothes, she hastened, still streaming, to make the acquaintance of her new domain. Since her religious sentiments were further developed than her aesthetic sensibility, Mademoiselle von Winckelried was enchanted by the highly Christian aspect of the site. She admired the great salon which the stained-glass windows filled with a mystical light, fingered the keys of the organ, swept through the bedchambers and kitchens like a whirlwind, and lingered in the chapel in order to thank the Lord for having recompensed her virtues in such wise. She vowed to consecrate this house to His glory and to make it a refuge for all whom Providence had not favoured as herself.

The Canoness von Winckelried was half mad, as has already been said, but she had a warm heart which no distress, provided it was picturesque, left indifferent. This residence, which Heaven had granted to her declining years, permitted her to realize late in life her most cherished dream: to harbour in her own home the derelicts of Society, those unfortunates whose follies and improvidence left them only the memory of a brilliant past, or else those whom some disgrace had exiled from their families. She already envisioned herself reigning over a court of *déclassé* baronesses, prima donnas surprised by old age, and ladies without honour whose wearied adventurers would keep them company under the verdant shade of her park.

Her desires were gratified more rapidly than she had expected, for no sooner was she settled upon the shores of the Traunsee than one of her childhood friends came to seek her hospitality. She had long been the mistress of the Prince of Galantha, whose sudden death now deprived her of all resource. She arrived in a delicious phaeton quilted in blue satin, the only trophy the Prince's heirs had allowed her to retain. Sophie von Winckelried realized at a glance that the carriage would render her considerable service on her rides through the country, and she embraced her friend effusively. Within several months, various guests came to live in the bedchambers she put at the disposal of celebrated unfortunates. One after another arrived: an Admiral in disgrace, an Archduchess morganatically married to a gypsy, an Anglican Bishop who composed operettas and his finest interpreter, a former diva of the Bouffes-Parisiens, a student from the University of Jena whose parents had cut him off, and last of all two ladies from the Empress's own household, driven from the Court following a scandal.

This little society lived for several months in an idyllic atmosphere. The Admiral valiantly leaned to the oars in order to tow the ladies over the lake. In the evenings, the gypsy took up his violin and accompanied the soprano, while the Bishop improvised chords on the organ. The fallen Highness insisted on being called Madame, and she was once again addressed in the third person. The two Viennese Countesses pursued their intrigues and laid a siege to the young student, who had eyes only for the concierge's daughter, a child of fifteen years.

All was for the best in the best of all possible *demi-mondes*, until the day that Mademoiselle von Winckelried gathered her friends together in the salon to inform them, quite solemnly, that she had no money left. Her brother the Coadjutor, indignant upon learning that she harboured under her roof an Anglican Bishop and other persons of dubious morality, had suppressed the pension he had granted her for over thirty years. This piece of news was received with insouciance.

"We have a roof. . . . That's the principal matter," murmured the Archduchess, who during the course of her adventurous existence had often encountered great difficulties remaining in hotels whose bills she could not pay.

"We have a park: let us transform it into a kitchen garden; it will permit us to survive. . . ." said the Bishop, who, like all Englishmen, was fond of gardening.

"The Admiral will fish in the lake, and I shall go hunting," declared the student.

"I do not wish to be a slacker: I shall seek an engagement at the Salzburg Opera. . . ." proposed the soprano in a faint voice.

"I have a certain gift for divining the future," announced one of the Empress's former ladies-in-waiting. "I predicted the death of His Imperial Highness Archduke Rudolf. . . ."

"And I excel in card tricks!" the other replied.

"We can tour the fairs and markets!" they rejoiced together. "Our takings will certainly be splendid!"

"No, no, my dear friends," the Canoness interrupted, "we shall not separate. Let us all remain here. In union there is strength, it is said. And perhaps fortunes as well. But we must find the means of earning some money without leaving this villa, which is so agreeable."

Thereupon a thousand projects were suggested, all of the most chimerical nature. It was proposed to open a gaming house, to run a *pension de famille*, to distil a liqueur from mountain herbs, or to raise Persian cats. The Archduchess offered to write her memoirs, but it was pointed out to the good creature that before her book brought in anything the entire little community might well have died of hunger. Nonetheless, this idea suggested another from which sprang a solution. The Bishop had completed a new operetta. He proposed to give a preview performance in the grand salon, and to invite to this spectacle all the notables of the region, who would certainly pay high prices for their seats.

"No, they won't come, or will refuse to pay!" exclaimed Mademoiselle von Winckelried. "But we must lure them here upon another pretext. We could give a charity *fête* in our own behalf. Of course we need not say that it is for ourselves! We shall invent, for the good of the cause, some worthy association: 'The Society for the Ransom of the Slavonians', for example, or that of the 'Fishermen's Widows'. . . ."

So much ingenuity was applauded, and for over a week its realization was discussed with the liveliest interest. The

Bishop, who insisted that his operetta be heard, consented to amputate two-thirds of it in order that the remaining portion be performed as a musical *divertissement* at the beginning of the afternoon. One of the Countesses seduced the Commander of the nearest garrison, who put at her disposal a fanfare of thirty musicians. The other transformed herself into a lady of charity; and all in black, her mouth as austere as the words that issued from it were persuasive, she visited the merchants of the surrounding localities in order to solicit their contributions. The phaeton was discovered to be too small to contain them all, and it was necessary to borrow a great hunting brake in order to bear in triumph to the villa some hundred objects. It was decided to put them up for a lottery. The Archduchess rummaged through her papers and discovered among them letters from a number of illustrious personages which she generously proposed to sell at auction. The former mistress of the Prince of Galantha recruited some dozen young girls from the countryside, who under her direction set to work making paper flowers. The student from Jena painted fantastic landscapes upon matchboxes. Each evening, the two Countesses plunged into a treatise on chiromancy, for they intended to disguise themselves as gypsies in order to tell fortunes. Only Mademoiselle von Winckelried had not yet found any particular activity for herself, and was in despair over the fact.

One afternoon, seated at her fireside, she was calmly reading the *Salzburg Gazette*, when her eyes were attracted by a heading upper case: "Courageous Exploit of Miss Flora Hammersmith, who flies over London in a balloon to distribute tracts." Miss Hammersmith was one of the first suffragettes whose campaigns were soon to agitate all of England.

"Now there," Mademoiselle von Winckelried immediately realized, "there is what I must do. It will be the crowning point of the fête!"

Since she was a Canoness, she considered that it would be

proper thus to illustrate the Assumption of the Blessed Virgin, and since she was cautious, she resolved to employ a captive balloon.

"From on high, I can rain down a shower of paper roses. It will be charming!"

She joined her guests downstairs in order to share this notion with them, and indeed they all judged it to be an admirable one.

"All the region will come to see it!" exclaimed the former mistress of the Prince of Galantha with enthusiasm.

"Why not represent instead the abduction of the Prophet Elias in a fiery chariot?" asked the Bishop. "Bengal lights could replace the flames, and would be in better taste than paper roses. Although I do not belong to your confession, I declare that the prospect of seeing the Virgin rising to Heaven in a balloon somewhat shocks me, and I fear that it would have a still stronger effect upon your guests. Moreover, certain disobliging remarks might be made apropos of this first choice, whereas I can readily see you as an Old Testament Prophet with a great white tunic and a long beard!"

"The Bishop is entirely right," the Archduchess approved. "You should wait for utter darkness in order to effect your ascent. Thus the mass of the balloon will not be visible, and only the gondola will be seen, transformed into a fiery chariot."

"And it will offer as well the advantage of obliging the crowd to remain longer—in other words, to eat and drink in order to occupy themselves. From a practical point of view, this detail is not a negligible one. . . ." the prima donna concluded.

The Canoness concurred with these opinions, and the student was dispatched to Vienna in order to rent a balloon with all its equipment.

A month later the final preparations were being completed. All the peasants from the neighbouring farms had come to lend their assistance. The park, decked out with some thirty tables loaded with victuals, presented a ravishing appearance. At each extremity of the central lawn stood a tent as sumptuous as those of the Grand Mogul. Inside, the two Countesses, veiled and gleaming with bits of glass and mirrors, waited for their customers. In the winter garden, a stand had been set up from which the student directed the auction sale of the autograph letters presented by the Archduchess. This latter was to assist Mademoiselle von Winckelried to do the honours of the estate. The star of the Bouffes-Parisiens shone with all her lustre and was administering the finishing touches to her costume in the tiny sacristy, transformed for the occasion into a *loge d'artiste*. With a troop of amateurs from Gmunden, she had rehearsed the Bishop's musical comedy more than twenty times, and felt herself prepared to scorch the salon's parquet. Upon the terrace was ranged the military fanfare, which had arrived that morning from Lambach. It was to play without interruption all afternoon and provide dance music for the young people. The Admiral had mustered at the villa's pier a flotilla which was in readiness to serve the pleasure of the strollers. Several young peasants, dressed in white from head to foot, were stationed at the oars. In the centre of a laurel bed the captive balloon was lying all in a heap. It was not to be filled until the last moment, in order to avoid wasting gas and disfiguring the park by its bulk.

The Canoness had already made several ascents in its gondola, and had declared herself satisfied with these experiments. The tombola prizes had been exhibited virtually everywhere, and several dozen little girls, suitably instructed by the Countesses, were prepared to sell tickets.

Towards noon, the first carriages were ranged near the stables. Of the two thousand persons to whom invitation cards had been dispatched, over four hundred had sent word they would attend the luncheon in the park, which was already a guarantee of success. The curiosity Sophie von Winckelried and her friends provoked throughout the region was so great that most people had eagerly seized this opportunity to visit the villa and obtain a glimpse of the strange beings it sheltered. The presence of the Archduchess exercised an irresistible attraction upon the petty nobility, who found it convenient to assume Court airs without having to go all the way to Vienna. Her scandalous reputation intrigued them so greatly that they came in hopes that she would abandon herself before their very eyes to some impropriety which would provide an excuse for gossip for years to come. They were a trifle disappointed not to find the Imperial Highness disguised as a bareback rider, but instead quite suitably attired in a grey taffeta gown embellished with mauve *passementerie*. She swayed a white parasol nobly overhead and gave her arm to the Canoness, who was dressed in an altogether extravagant crinoline. A bonnet of pink satin framed her radiant face. She pressed to her bosom an asthmatic Italian greyhound whose blue tongue greedily lapped at all hands that came within reach.

Luncheon at the little tables was a triumph. The Archduchess's morganatic husband conducted the fanfare with a masterful baton. The theatrical performance which followed scored a lively success. The applause and the encores demanded by the spectators avenged the Star for the obscurity to which her liaison with the Bishop had condemned her. Matters proceeded in this happy fashion until about five o'clock, when harbingers of a storm began to make the atmosphere oppressive.

Ladies, constricted in their whaleboned gowns, wished to seek a little coolness on the lake, and asked the young sailors to row them out to an islet situated not far from shore. They lingered there so long that still other ladies, crowded upon the tiny wharf in the expectation of their return, spoke openly of sending the captain of the local *gendarmerie* to draw up a report of these nautical diversions.

During this time certain old gentlemen, apparently eager to win all the prizes of the tombola under the best circumstances, bargained for the tickets in so pressing a manner that some of the young salesgirls, bewildered, had burst into tears. Others, more courageous, were engaging in their first sparring bouts.

In the darkness of their tents, the two Countesses indulged themselves to their hearts' content, and predicted the most alarming misadventures to their customers. The President of the High Court of Justice and the most important landholder of the region heard themselves told that they would end their days, the former on the scaffold, the latter in Potter's Field.

The Countess de Marchfield, an octogenarian lady, learned with stupefaction that she would soon have sentimental difficulties, for her lover, it seemed, was about to leave her. Young Baroness Ferenczy, married only lately, was warned that her husband was deceiving her with her chambermaid. These singular revelations created a certain malaise which increased as the clouds continued to accumulate around the summit of the Traunstein. The Archduchess, intoxicated by the homage of the squireens, recounted with the most daring commentaries the vicissitudes of her marriage and boasted of the gypsy's amorous exploits. Mademoiselle von Winckelried, who was wandering from group to group, heard her somewhat raucous voice exclaiming: "What a bow stroke he has, if you could imagine, *ma chère*! In his arms, I am nothing more than a trembling violin. . . ."

The thirty soldiers were playing wild mazurkas that electrified the dancers. The Bishop, discretion thrown to the winds, whirled about with the diva. The Baron de Zippe's crimson face and white sideburns emerged from a swirl of skirts that revealed the admirable legs of the Princess von Thalsen, whose recent widowhood did not appear to have saddened her in the slightest. Mademoiselle von Winckelried overheard remarks quite as daring as those of the Archduchess.

"What odd behaviour for a Papal Chamberlain!" exclaimed a young woman struggling in the arms of her cavalier, who was trying to drag her into the depths of the park.

"You forget that I am also Virilist of the Diet of Croatia!" the latter replied.

With what little good sense she had left, Mademoiselle von Winckelried realized that the *fête* would turn into a bacchanale if she failed to find means of restoring it to order. There was no better one than that of advancing the Biblical figuration, which was scheduled to take place only at nightfall. The increasingly sombre masses of clouds were already creating a penumbra which accelerated the daylight's decline. The Canoness gave orders to fill the balloon. Its silhouette rose slowly above the laurels, like a black moon. Soon the crowd flowed towards the lawns in order to observe the spectacle. The musicians had ceased, and the silence that suddenly reigned permitted all to hear the rolls of thunder, echoed by the mountainside. A kind of anguish seized the spectators. The ladies who had visited the islet had just returned, and were fanning themselves nervously. Their mariners had vanished, which plunged the Canoness into embarrassment, for she counted on their help to manœuvre the balloon's departure. The latter continued to swell and had nearly reached the treetops. The old gentlemen, exhausted, regarded all these preparations with uncertainty. The Countess de Marchfield was warning them against the dangers of an explosion.

"When I was still a child," she said, "Montgolfier balloons had been launched upon the entry of the French into Vienna, and one of these . . ."

A louder rumbling interrupted her; she crossed herself. The storm was growing closer. The Canoness saw certain persons demanding their carriages: she would have to make haste. She put on the long white tunic and fastened the false beard, by means of which, the darkness playing its part, she might pass for the Prophet Elias. She climbed into the gondola, assured herself that the wicks of the Bengal lights were in readiness, and lit them.

"Let slip the moorings!" she cried heroically.

The balloon shuddered faintly, but did not rise. Someone

had forgotten to untie the hawsers of the ballast sacks. Already the Bengal lights were exploding in many-coloured sheaves. Without a moment's hesitation, Mademoiselle von Winckelried seized the axe which was among the instruments in the gondola and severed the cables. The balloon rose some thirty yards, and she heard the salvoes of applause exploding beneath her. With her axe, she cut the last of the sandbag ropes. One of them, of a larger diameter, gave her more difficulties than the rest, but she succeeded at last and noticed with satisfaction that the balloon immediately gained altitude. Upon leaning over the edge of her blazing gondola, she perceived the Gothic bell-tower of her villa, the livid surface of the lake, and the Gmunden road upon which the carriage lamps trembled like fireflies. The last Bengal lights went out, and darkness suddenly enveloped her. Great flashes cleaved the heavens, and the rolls of thunder grew ever more threatening. Gusts of wind shook the balloon and made the gondola quite uncomfortable for an elderly lady. After several moments, she was amazed to be drifting still, at the mercy of the elements.

"How enormously long that cable must be. . . ." she murmured, thinking of the line that attached her to earth.

She bent over the gondola's edge once more in order to examine its fastenings: no cable connected her to the earth. The lake was no more than a silvery speck, touched by a slanting ray that had just pierced through a rent in the clouds. The Traunstein had vanished. Wild with terror, the Canoness began to cry. The first raindrops replaced upon her face the tears which her eyes, dilated by fear, could no longer shed. The tempest was driving her in the direction of a city whose lights sparkled a thousand feet below her. She tried in vain to work the safety valve. The balloon's disordered oscillations had caught the cord in a mesh of the netting. She realized then that all was lost, and fainted before having been able to commend her soul to God, towards Whom she was mounting at a speed of twenty-five leagues an hour.

The gondola and the guide rope were recovered near a village of the Sandjak of Novibaza. The balloon's envelope was fished out of the Adriatic by an aviso of the Montenegran fleet, which, having taken it for the Great Sea Serpent, cannonaded it with red-hot bullets for over three hours. As for the Canoness von Winckelried, no one ever saw her again. She has become one of the legends of the Traunsee, and on certain stormy nights, when the clouds are amassed about the mountaintop, there is always one, rounder and darker than the rest, which, after having hovered above the lake for a moment, rises towards the horizon like, of yore, the Canoness's balloon.

The Divine Baroness

■ ■ ■ COUNT OTTO LANDECK, whose adventures had been ■ ■ ■ myriad, delighted in recounting this one:

At eighteen years of age I left Dresden, where my family resided, to study architecture in Rome. My parents, who were in modest circumstances, had furnished me, rather than money, with letters of introduction to various members of Roman Society whom they had met upon their wedding journey. My grandmother, for her part, had enjoined me to visit one of her childhood friends whom she had not seen for over sixty years but with whom she maintained an episodic correspondence. I promised all that was asked of me, but I must confess that no sooner had I arrived in Rome than I yielded to the spell of the South so completely I forgot all my resolutions, not excepting that of working diligently to obtain my certificate. I had registered in a studio which I lost no time abandoning in order to attend that school of the *pittoresco* which is to be found in the spectacle of the streets. I spent my days strolling across the piazzas or through the alleyways; I engaged in conversation with whatever strangers chance afforded: flower-girls, artisans, beadles. When the weather was too warm, I sought refuge on the terrace of some café or, to save the price of refreshments, in a museum, where the paintings afforded me the illusion of a luxury my own life could no longer sustain.

This Bohemian existence lasted several months, until the winter arrived, and for all my insouciance I found myself sensitive to the cold. I had rented, on the top floor of a dilapidated *palazzo*, an enormous *alsa*, which served me as studio and bed-chamber alike. It was lit by three large windows through whose ill-fitting panes whistled the Roman wind, sharp and icy as no other. On certain days I was too cold to work, and preferred to remain in my bed, where—forgive me this detail, but it has its significance, as you shall discover in the sequel—I was frequently joined by a young fruitgirl upon whose favours I had, indeed, dissipated my last resources. Grateful or pitying, it was now she who was keeping me. The pretty creature would come to me once she had sold her fruits, bringing with her the rudiments of a luncheon which we would share. I was too young or too heedless to feel any shame at this situation, and deplored only the fact that I had been reduced to such an extremity.

In order to escape from it, and to improve my usual fare somewhat, I decided to pay some calls upon my parents' former connections, whom I had hitherto neglected in the euphoria of my new-found independence. Most of these good people were in the cemetery, and it was merely for conscience' sake that I inquired the whereabouts of the villa of the Baroness de Krimml, my grandmother's friend from her convent days. It was immediately described to me—the Baroness appeared to be quite well known—and one February afternoon in 1908 I was shown by an Arab major-domo into a salon where the potted palms interlaced their fronds after the fashion of the period. In the centre of the room a fountain murmured in its white marble shell. I had no time to examine this décor further, for the Baroness de Krimml made her entrance, preceded by two Pekinese that burst into furious yapping as soon as they saw me. With her flesh-tinted veils and her enormous jewels, she resembled some Oriental priestess, or perhaps an ancient idol embellished by her worshippers. She fluttered her draperies and made her bracelets click as she twittered some words of welcome whose enthusiastic intonation seemed to me to bode well.

"My dear Stéphanie's grandson!" she repeated, uttering tiny chirps of joy to which the yapping of her dogs furnished an echo.

Thereupon she opened her arms in a theatrical gesture, and I threw myself into them, enchanted. The Baroness pleased me beyond description. Ten minutes later, sitting down to a copious tea, I was telling the amiable lady my adventures while she, her eyes shining with pleasure, observed:

"We are going to understand one another very well!"

As a matter of fact, less than a month after this first visit, I had advanced far into her good graces, and was enjoying myself tremendously. I had found in the Baroness a mother and an accomplice, a friend and a confidante. She had asked to meet Amalia, my fond mistress, and one morning had had her coachman drive her all the way to the Piazza Fiametta, where she had bought out the girl's tray. She expressed nothing but indulgence for this liaison of mine, and subsequently, by daily purchases, discreetly favoured my passion. The old lady had made a conquest of Amalia as well. The three of us were all tenderness and sentiment, and I was making plans for the future.

The Baroness, you see, had never had a child, no doubt in order not to discredit her husband, who, as a Knight of Malta, had been obliged to take a vow of chastity. Her affections had hitherto been expended upon her absurd dogs, a sleepy chaplain and the gardener's granddaughter. She spoilt them all with comfits taken from splendid candy-boxes signed by Fabergé. She also cultivated several exotic goldfish that resembled her Pekinese, and of which she would say, with a throb of emotion in her voice:

"You cannot conceive how affectionate these creatures are. . . ."

In a matter of weeks I had become the darling of the house; I acquired precedence over the dogs and the gardener's granddaughter, and my only rival, a ruined nobleman who pursued the Baroness with his mercenary attentions, had been shown the door.

"You are too old, my poor friend!" she remarked to this suitor twenty years her junior.

As for the Abbé, he sanctioned by his respectful silence this chaste and unexpected idyll of ours. He must have seen many others! Three or four times a week I lunched or dined at the Villa Paraliccio. In a mysterious basement a French cook elaborated wonderful dishes that offered an agreeable respite from the menus of cheap restaurants or from the frugality of Amalia's repasts. Since I mention the latter's name, I must add that my attachment to her person had lost its intensity. The shadow of a sordid reality was sadly tarnishing the colours of our intimacy. In order to justify myself in my own eyes, I would gaily sing this refrain from *La Périchole*:

> *Peut-on vraiment s'aimer*
> *Lorsque l'on meurt de faim?*

for the *vie de Bohème* I was leading seemed to me infinitely less picturesque than formerly. I preferred to it the *vie de château* I enjoyed with the divine Baroness. Often, in the afternoons, we would make an expedition in an old two-horse barouche which she maintained in order not to grieve her coachman, who detested automobiles. In order to face the open air, she swathed herself in tremulous feather boas and light gauzes that quivered at the least touch of wind, and she wore enough jewels to compete in clinks and tinkles with the harness bells of the team. In this fashion we would visit the city's famous sites or take tea in some fashonable hotel. At first, our grand entrances in lobbies, filled with spiteful and idle crowds, embarrassed me a trifle. The notion that these people must have formed of the bizarre couple we surely appeared, the Baroness leaning on my arm, brought a blush of confusion to my face. Yet I could scarcely say to her: "Sit here, Mother!" in order to save appearances.

She must have divined my discomfort, for one day she said to me: "Just call me Tante Nada and *honi soit qui mal y pense!*"

Moreover, she was quite oblivious to other people's opinions, and offered her own with blithe indifference to convention. Consequently she had quarrelled with half of the *monde noir* and three-quarters of the *monde rouge*, which explained, more than her circumstances as a widow—indeed, a merry one—the solitude in which I found her living. The only guests at the Villa Paraliccio were foreign friends whose presence awakened in me an obscure jealousy. She received seldom, fortunately, and lived more in the company of the dead than in that of the living. Her favourite pastime was the reading of royal biographies. She expended more attention upon the photographs of sovereigns, enthroned in state on her piano, than upon the admirable paintings the villa contained, and the *Almanach de Gotha* was her preferred bedtime reading. It was, moreover, constantly at hand in order to supply some lacuna in her memory, and wrought wondrous order in the chaos of princely genealogies. The major portion of her day was devoted to correspondence. The letters she received were scrupulously kept beneath the cushions of the grand salon. There were as many armchairs here as there were titled correspondents. If, in the course of conversation, the name of one of these had just been mentioned, the dear Baroness sprang up and drew the astonished visitor to her feet, who had no idea he was sitting precisely on the latest letter from the Archduchess Annunziata, which she forthwith proceeded to read. Such frivolity did not prevent my new friend from being a woman of judgment, as she proved to me when Amalia, transformed into a maenad, informed me with tears and sobs that she was expecting a "*piccolo bambino*" of which, apparently, I was the father. She had come to share this good news with me one evening, at the very moment I was dressing to dine at the Villa Paraliccio. As you may imagine, her information completely spoilt my appetite. The Baroness noticed as much and plied me with questions. It was not long before I had revealed to her the extent of my misfortune.

"You must not hesitate a moment," she replied. "You shall stay here tonight, and tomorrow we shall send the coachman to remove your things. You do not know Italian customs. . . . At dawn your apartment will be invaded by a greedy family, eager to take every advantage of the dishonour that has fallen upon it. A father, drunk with rage, will threaten your life. A mother who has been dead for ten years will resuscitate in order to curse you with torrents of blasphemy and invocations to all the Saints of the calendar. Countless brothers will appear from the depths of Calabria to avenge their sister's virtue, while living at your expense. A grandmother will be borrowed from the neighbours in order to add a note of respectability to this family portrait, and you will not escape these people's hands without having married the girl or promised her an income which will ruin you for life."

This description alarmed me so thoroughly that I did not hesitate to accept the Baroness's hospitality in order to flee such an outpouring of outraged sentiments, and I established my residence at the Villa Paraliccio. Amalia's parents received a visit from the Baroness de Krimml, who bargained at length with them for the price of their silence. I do not know what they asked of her, and I was frivolous enough to wish to know nothing of a transaction whose stake and staple I had become. Once the affair was settled, I belonged, in effect, to the divine Baroness. Yet far from abusing her power, she contrived a thousand ways of making me forget it. Life continued in this delicious fashion, and I ended by feeling towards this old lady an emotion far more profound than that which had formerly pressed me into Amalia'a arms. She was always so gay, so original! Her conversation was so lively, so witty! I loved her persistent youthfulness, her naughty child's laugh, her way of trotting along with quick, light steps, her arms thrown back a trifle, as though she were about to take wing; and I also loved, to be candid, her immense fortune. Everything about her gratified my heart's desires. In order to content those of the flesh, one could always resort to adventures in Rome's ill-famed alleyways, and on certain evenings I set off on expeditions whose description, the following morning, constituted Tante Nada's delight. She called them *"les jolies parties en passant"*. I had difficulty enjoying my happiness to the full, so natural did it seem to me; I was accustomed to the extraordinary. My present state was cloudless, and my future promised to be the same, for Tante Nada had not concealed from me the fact that she would take steps to assure its comfort. The child which was the fruit of my relations with Amalia had been sent to a village nurse in the Abruzzi. All my anxiety on that account had vanished. How could I have guessed that this tranquillity would be destroyed by an event so astonishing and, in particular, so strange that it was truly impossible to foresee its consequences? On the contrary, it first appeared to me as the crowning touch of my happiness.

One day, when remorse at having abandoned my architectural studies had inspired me to return to the studio, I made the acquaintance there of a ravishing American girl whose name I shall not disclose, for she subsequently married one of her nation's most celebrated statesmen. I was so charmed by her poetic beauty that I fell in love with her enough to return to my work. Henceforth, I was to be seen at the studio every morning. After paying a discreet and silent court for some time, I emboldened myself sufficiently to invite her to tea. With that freedom of manner which masks, in American girls, a certain austerity of behaviour, she accepted my offer quite naturally. I am unable to say precisely why I had kept the secret of this new passion from the Baroness, perhaps because I attached too little importance to it at the beginning and too much thereafter. I apprised Florence that I was staying with an old relative who lived sequestered from the world, and she showed no surprise at not being invited to the villa.

Never had I been so capitvated. Rome revealed itself to me as a different city. I spent afternoons of a matchless felicity exploring with Florence the streets, the piazzas, the ruins that I had formerly wandered over in search of more vulgar pleasures. Since I could not make my way into the convent where she had taken lodgings, we spent our time out of doors, and exchanged confidences in the less frequented rooms of museums. Thus I could at least describe, during my evenings with the Baroness, the masterpieces of painting or sculpture of which I had vaguely been aware while kissing Florence. This double life lasted until the day I asked the lovely American to marry me. I did not conceal from the girl that my only fortune was an age-old heritage of family virtues, among whose number economy did not figure. She was an orphan, and I knew that her guardian, delighted to be rid of his charge, would unconditionally approve whatever choice she should make. Florence asked me for a week in which to reflect, and finally replied that she accepted my suit. I wrote to Dresden to seek the consent of my parents, and then I decided to announce the news to Tante Nada. I rather feared that she would not forgive my dissimulation, and was apprehensive about the effects of my tardy confession. To my great relief, the Baroness, if she revealed some surprise, showed no displeasure whatever, and instead of reproaching me for my silence, congratulated me on having been able to keep my secret.

"And have you kept that of your liaison with the little fruit-girl in the Piazza Fiametta as well?" she asked me with a smile.

"Yes," I replied with some embarrassment.

"It is better so. You are now about to begin your life anew; but," she added with a malicious air, "perhaps you will regret it some day. . . ."

She wished to meet Florence, and invited her to dinner early the following week. I felt a great weight lifted from my mind. Tante Nada had not seemed disappointed or jealous, and was eager to accord the warmest possible reception to the woman whom I already regarded as my wife. She told me she was preparing a surprise for my betrothed, by which I under-

stood that she would present her with the splendid pearl necklace I had several times admired in her jewel case.

The barouche was sent around to call for Florence at her
convent. To win the old lady's sympathies, my fiancée had
dressed with particular care, and upon seeing her step down
from the carriage I could not resist the pleasure of embracing
her, so charming did she appear. The Baroness de Krimml
hurried forward to meet her, greeted her most affectionately as
her daughter-to-be and pressed her to a bosom armoured with
amethysts. She had crowned her periwig with white roses and
was wearing the most extravagant of her gowns, the one she
reserved for the reception of royalty in exile. The Pekinese
dashed forward with happy barks and leaped unceremoniously upon Florence's knees the instant she sat down. I was
enchanted. Dinner was served a few moments later, and we
proceeded to table. As an entrée, there was a golden-brown
soufflé which was so hot that no sooner had I swallowed the
first bite than I drank off a tremendous glass of water at one
mouthful. This was the moment the Baroness chose to tell me,
pointing to the fruits that decorated the centre of the table:

"This afternoon, I happened to meet that little fruit-seller
you abandoned. How sorry I felt for the poor girl! I saw her
child, who has come back from the country. He resembled
you. . . ."

My glass slipped from my hand and fell upon my plate,
where it broke into a thousand pieces. The water splashed onto
the tablecloth. Imperturbably, the major-domo changed my
napery. Florence, who stared at us uncomprehendingly, paled
upon seeing my guilty expression. The Baroness smiled
serenely.

"Yes," she continued. "You should at least have recognized
the child, since you wouldn't marry its mother."

I stammered:

"Tante Nada . . . Tante Nada. . ."

She turned amiably towards Florence and explained, in that light and detached tone one employs to enable someone who has not followed the conversation to be *au courant*, that I had seduced and forsaken an unfortunate creature who was dying of love for me.

I did not know whether I should insult the Baroness, strike her, silence her by force, or stand up, drag Florence from the table and leave the house. I said nothing, staring stupidly at the samovar that gleamed on the mantelpiece. I had the feeling of living several moments in the life of another person, and felt myself to be strangely detached from all that surrounded me. Hence, in a semi-trance, the mind wanders unbeknownst to the body which no longer obeys its behests. Suddenly, I came to my senses. Florence's voice rang in my ears.

"Is this true?" she asked, her voice low and choked.

Horror and incredulity were to be read upon her countenance. This touched me more than the Baroness's remarks. The die was cast.

"Yes, it is true!" I exclaimed.

And, pushing back my chair, I reached the door, leaving the two of them together.

I walked all night through the streets of Rome, wild with fury, with grief and also with rancour at having been so cruelly abused as to the cursed Baroness's true sentiments. In the morning, I sought refuge with a friend who took me in for several days and loaned me the money necessary to return to Dresden. It was in this fashion that there vanished at one and the same moment from my life the Baroness de Krimml and Florence, yet it is the former, I believe, whom I most regret. . . .

Of Love and Money

■ ■ ■ THERE ONCE WAS A NOBLE and illustrious family that ■ ■ ■ lived in northern Moravia, revelling in luxury, godlessness and scorn of its neighbours. The de Träxerns were Austrians who had come to Poland at the time of the first partitions. They had remained ever since, and despite every effort on the part of the region's inhabitants they never abandoned the Siérakov estates, which they had seized. Taking advantage of the political upheavals of the nineteenth century, they had even managed to enlarge their holdings considerably, thereby effecting a similar increase of their unpopularity as well.

By 1900 the Château of Siérakov, the masterpiece of the architect Bernardo Merettini, was the residence of the Counts Roman and Adam de Träxern, twin brothers whose resemblance to one another was so perfect that when one of them married no one had ever been able to decide which of the two it was. They were universally taken for each other by all who had dealings with them, and spiteful tongues declared that the new Countess de Träxern was no exception among the latter. This twofold confusion, however, had produced only one child, a sad and sickly boy whose precocious misadventures suggested those of the doll in *Les Malheurs de Sophie*.

At the age of five he had fallen from a window of the château, and in consequence one of his legs remained shorter than the other. When he was eight a clumsy serving-maid had upset a teapot on his head, which rendered him almost entirely bald, and deaf in one ear as well. At eleven he had contracted the smallpox, at thirteen had fallen from a horse, and finally, upon turning fifteen, had been seized with nervous convulsions so severe that even the physicians from Vienna confessed themselves powerless. On each of these occasions Madame de Träxern had wept bitter tears but these had not kept her son from becoming, in succession, lame, bald, deaf, disfigured and virtually epileptic. Her husband's death, followed by that of her brother-in-law, removed all hopes of providing the de Träxerns a more suitable representative, and so it came to pass that the future of their race, and indeed the fate of their fortune, rested upon the unhappy Léonard, who was as incapable of insuring the one as of expending the other. He was an unsociable youth, misanthropic and misogynist, and rarely left his bedchamber, where his English nursemaid was forever reading him Perrault's fairy-tales. He loved the story of *Riquet à la Houppe*, cherishing in his secret heart the hope that some miracle would one day transform him into a gallant cavalier.

Not many leagues from the splendours of Siérakov there lived in straitened circumstances a young Pole of ancient stock who had only his handsome face for his fortune, his father having taken it upon himself to throw to the winds the last resources of a patrimony already considerably diminished by political confiscations. Reversing the Gospel phrase, one might have said of Count Vladislaf Ratkovitz that the spirit was weak but the flesh was willing, and in order to finance his sentimental extravagances he was at last obliged to sell Balanovka, his château. With his entire family, he had taken refuge in a kind of hunting lodge, where he led a most precarious existence. His son Mathias, who loved luxury, gaiety and adventures, deplored this situation.

"What is the use of being well made," he lamented, "what is the use of being handsome if one is poor and must inhabit a forsaken wilderness such as this?"

"What is the use of being rich, if one is an object of pity or horror to the world?" Léonard de Träxern was sighing, wondering whether he should throw himself out of his bedroom window once again.

The meeting of these two beings transformed their destinies. It was, like many important events, the work of chance. On one of his solitary walks, during which he was in the habit of laying the most ambitious plans, Mathias Ratkovitz encountered the Countess de Träxern, who had turned her ankle in falling from her horse. Mathias helped her back into the saddle and accompanied her as far as Siérakov, which he had always admired from a distance, through a curtain of trees. He was asked inside to rest and take some refreshment, an invitation which did not need to be repeated. His unexpected arrival did not afford Léonard an opportunity to run away as he was in the habit of doing when any stranger appeared. He stopped, petrified, and imagined he had had a vision: never had he seen so beautiful a being!

Mathias Ratkovitz resembled those delicate models which were the delight of the Pre-Raphaelites or of Ruskin's aesthetic disciples. He had regular features, golden hair and a visionary gaze like that of the early Christians. His excessively slender and arched waist, his overly delicate hands, his too gentle voice made him seem a trifle affected. Handsome at twenty, he would be ridiculous at forty, for his youth threatened to persist. If Léonard was dazzled by this marvellous apparition, Mathias was stupefied in his turn by the sumptuous comforts of Siérakov. He was therefore delighted to accept the luncheon invitation which Madame de Träxern, pleased to see her awkward son growing tractable, extended to him for a day of the following week. This was the beginning of a celebrated friendship which was to constitute the wonder, the scandal and the entertainment of the whole province. It was the union of the blind man and the paralytic. Mathias found at Siérakov the opulent way of life of which he had always dreamed; Léonard congratulated himself upon a friend whose beauty allowed him to forget his own ugliness. Looking at Mathias, he seemed to see, as in a magical mirror, the reflection of the face he ideally wished to possess, and on certain days he no longer doubted that Heaven, answering his secret longings at last, had made him the object of some mysterious metamorphosis.

Little by little Mathias grew used to coming to Siérakov and spending all his days with his new friend. They were seen strolling together through the grounds, chattering animatedly upon the river bank or rushing along the roads by bicycle, a sport for which Léonard had discovered the liveliest enthusiasm. He bestowed one of those vehicles upon Mathias, seizing every pretext to confer presents which might bind the beautiful creature to him more closely. He even went so far as to pay his gambling debts, or those which he contracted, with a deplorable heedlessness, among the tradesmen of the nearby town. By the year's end, yielding to Léonard's entreaties, Mathias finally took up residence at Siérakov altogether, where an apartment of his own had been provided for him. Nevertheless, this perpetual intimacy, Léonard's exclusive and jealous affection, oppressed him without his daring to disclose just how burdensome he found it. He was flattered to provoke such ardent sentiments, but found their manifestations somewhat tyrannical and knew not what to reply to his friend when the latter, employing the mystical language of which he was so fond, called him "his true life" or "his beloved". He suffered great pains to keep from smiling at, and still greater to respond to, such enthusiasm. Yet he was fond of Léonard, though his affection consisted only of gratitude and pity: it was as deficient in warmth as it was in spontaneity. The young Austrian, whose solitude and trials had developed his psychological capacities, soon perceived this fact. It inspired in him a certain vexation, and he lavished his ingenuity upon keeping Mathias with him by every means within his power. No sooner did he divine the least slackening, the slightest velleity of independence, than he fell into a violent despair, threatened to kill himself and finally obliged Mathias to swear a solemn oath never to leave him. Thus Mathias, who would have promised anything in the world to escape his family's sordid existence, was beginning to regret his promise. Once again he lamented the waste of his youth all for the satisfaction of a capricious, egotistial and unsociable weakling. Despite all his suggestions, Léonard had refused to leave Siérakov to live in Vienna. He feared the world in which his physical aspect prohibited him from appearing to advantage, and now that he had caught this rare bird he was reluctant to risk letting the lovely creature escape.

Necessity engenders resourcefulness. Mathias Ratkovitz, who was seeking to rid himself of this servitude while retaining its material advantages, then conceived an idea which he considered heaven-sent. One day, when Léonard was repeating to him for the hundredth time that he loved him more than all the world, Mathias assumed a grave expression and replied that such friendship, far from constituting the admiration of Society by its ardour and constancy, furnished occasion for the most insulting gossip. Considering the severity of public opinion in their regard, Mathias wondered whether it might not be more prudent, in their mutual interests, to separate for a time. Léonard grew pale.

"What people think cannot matter to us!" he exclaimed. "We alone signify in this matter, and we are happy, are we not?"

"Indeed we are," the handsome Mathias hastened to declare, "but I have a family—parents, brothers, a sister—who have been troubled by such spiteful remarks, and I must think of them. . . . You know that where I am concerned these things have no importance—I am above such scandal—but in my sister's case, for instance, I must yield before public opinion. . . ."

It was indeed the first time that Mathias Ratkovitz had thus given himself a moment's concern over a sister whom he detested, but he had just discovered that she might furnish him the means to accomplish his secret intention. Mademoiselle Hedwige Ratkovitz was in every detail the contrary of her brother. Old for her years, as crabbed of temper as she was critical, she was an austere creature, inimical to luxury and frivolity. Like most ugly women, she was possessed of an aggressive virginity, and she believed herself continually subject to the brutal lust of men. To safeguard charms which no one would have had the temerity to threaten, she had adopted a severe, surly and spiteful attitude towards the stronger sex.

"I have no great fondness for fops!" she frequently asserted to her friends, who suspected her, quite unjustly, moreover, of finding the grapes too green. In any case, men found her too ripe and hitherto none of their number had dreamed of seeking her hand. Ugly, angular and impoverished, but as indefatigable in her piety as a Salvation Army sister, Hedwige Ratkovitz, it suddenly occurred to her brother, was the ideal wife for the wretched but rich Léonard. She could take care of him, and her presence at Siérakov would silence spiteful tongues, while permitting Mathias to absent himself occasionally on the pretext of discretion. This union would also have the advantage of rescuing the Ratkovitz family from the difficult circumstances in which they languished, for the Count de Träxern could hardly fail to assure his relations by marriage a suitable style of life.

And so it was that little by little he convinced his friend, who had no such intention or desire, to marry his sister. When Léonard confessed that Nature had shown herself much less generous in his regard than Fortune, Mathias had replied lightly that a marriage of pure convenience had no need to be consummated. Though relieved on this delicate point, Léonard had raised all kinds of objections. He was not at all pleased by the prospect of his friend's entire family taking up residence at Siérakov; he scented a trap and resisted all Mathias' cajolery that was intended to make him fall into it. At this juncture the Countess de Träxern, who had favoured the project, passed away, and her grief-stricken son let his consent be wrung from him.

Mathias fell upon his neck.

"How happy we shall all be together! We shall never part from one another!" he exclaimed, already thinking of the fashion in which he would occupy his time during the new couple's wedding journey.

On account of Léonard's recent bereavement the betrothal ceremony took place in intimate circumstances. Hedwige Ratkovitz became chatelaine of Siérakov, to the great surprise of the region, which had known nothing of this affair, and to her own astonishment as well, for she had scarcely been consulted. Yet she raised no obstacle, happy as she was to insure, by her sacrifice, her parents' declining years. She declared naïvely that she did not consider Léonard so ugly. Mathias had been considerably relieved to find that matters were falling out so well, for he had feared that his sister, suspecting the true nature of the transaction, would refuse to be a party to it. Léonard had shown himself less accommodating during the drawing-up of the contract by which he accorded Hedwige an enormous dowry and signed over to his brother-in-law the revenue the latter desired. He had attempted to argue, but a smile from Mathias had persuaded him. On the other hand, he remained adamant on the subject of the wedding journey. Mathias had broached the notion of a world tour, but Léonard, who feared to be left alone with his wife, would not even hear of a visit to the city of Vienna. He would consent to no more than a visit to several châteaux in the vicinity.

They caused a sensation. The splendour of their equipage, selected by Mathias, contrasted strikingly with the unfortunate aspect of their persons. Léonard—tiny, glum, misshapen—limped on the arm of his wife, who towered above him by at least a head and who, with her Salvationist carriage, seemed to be the governess of an old goblin hard pressed by misfortunes. This strange couple inspired smiles, but the smiles changed to open merriment when, some months later, curious rumours began circulating concerning the conjugal life of the seigneurs of Siérakov. The austere, cold and gaunt Hedwige was undergoing a metamorphosis. She began to bloom, acquiring weight, colour and . . . temperament! This was the consequence of her new style of life: fine meals, select wines, calm naps in the conservatory with its flowers and their heady perfumes—all awakened in her certain vague and tender ideas by which she was the first to be amazed. The library of the château contained many novels. To beguile her idleness and dispel the foolish notions that befogged her brain, she read a number of them, chosen at random. She thus discovered the nature of the agitation to which she had fallen a victim: she was, quite simply, in love with her husband. This ungainly, timid and fugitive creature pleased her; she was fond of his scanty hair, his grotesque figure and his pockmarked face. She desired to touch him, to caress him, as much out of curiosity as from the sincere desire to prove her love and gratitude to a man who had rescued her from penury. She was still ignorant of the hidden purpose Mathias had pursued in marrying her off, but since she was in the habit of regarding all his designs with mistrust, she now suspected him of some infernal machination of which her husband or herself might be the victim.

During the first weeks of her marriage she found it quite natural that Léonard, after distractedly kissing her hand, should leave her at the door of her bedchamber each evening, but ever since her readings had given her a greater experience of real life, her husband's indifference grieved at the same time that it alarmed her. A honeymoon, she had learned, was an enchantment during which the lovers never left one another's arms and exhausted themselves in the thousand ways and wiles of love. Such things, it is true, generally occurred under exotic skies. Perhaps, in her husband's coldness, climate had played its part! She found herself a prey to a burning nostalgia for Venice, land of lovers, and longed to journey there with Léonard. She would thereby dissipate the influence her brother exerted over him and of which she felt a certain jealousy, coupled with a degree of bitterness. The attentions he showered upon Mathias and not upon her shocked Hedwige. The signs of affection her husband lavished upon his brother-in-law offended her. One day she surprised Léonard leaning on her brother's shoulder, one arm around his neck, and a part of the truth appeared to her. She had always despised Mathias; henceforth she hated him. She wished to rid herself of his hateful presence, but to her stupefaction it was her husband who opposed her wishes. This second discovery mortified Hedwige, and her sufferings multiplied therefrom: it was not so much a question of attacking her brother as of attempting the conquest of her own husband.

She resolved to devote her energies to this enterprise. Why should she not succeed? Other women had done so before herself. She would make use of their strategems. Perhaps Léonard, conscious of his physical inadequacies, dared not manifest his true feelings, fearing lest they be ill-received. . . . She must encourage him. She sent to Paris for costly gowns and essayed *décolletés* which made her servants smile. Neither her brother nor her husband seemed to take any notice of them. She inundated herself with violent perfumes. The major-domo sneezed as he offered the courses at dinner, but the two friends did not appear to be discommoded. At table, moreover, they quite excluded her from their conversation and after each repast withdrew into one or the other's apartments in order to chat together. Observing that her husband remained unconscious of all her attempts at seduction, Hedwige de Träxern determined to employ more direct methods. If a married woman's state involved many duties, it also promised certain rights: was not one of them *being loved*? She contrived to separate her husband from her brother as often as possible, which was all the easier since the latter asked for nothing better than to make good his escape. The moment she found herself alone with Léonard, Hedwige multiplied occasions to brush against him, to lean over him. She inquired after his health, took his hand to see if he were suffering from fever, caressed his brow to dispel the headache, and each time she managed to touch him tremors ran through her frame as if she had had a fit. If he appeared unexpectedly, her heart beat harder, her blood boiled in her veins, her tongue stumbled over her words and she felt herself about to faint. At first, she had feared she was a victim of the sort of guilty passion the Church reproves, and she had made the journey to Cracov to consult an old priest whom she trusted completely. The worthy religious had reassured her, and prophesied that with God's help victory was certain. To bring matters to a head, the Countess de Träxern, enflamed with the love of God and that of her husband, resolved to strike a decisive blow. One of her friends, to whom she had confided her torments, had given her the idea.

"Only consider, my dear," this companion had remarked, "your husband is timid with you because he has apparently had no experience of women. His is a delicate spirit which faints before the material aspects of life and seeks refuge in the realm of abstraction. You must . . . force his hand, if I may use such an expression. A man should never marry before having had several mistresses, which gives him the superiority of experience over us, pure brides as we are. In Léonard's case, in order to vanquish his apprehension, you should confront him with a *fait accompli*, or, rather, with a *fait* to be *accompli*. . . . My dear, why don't you put yourself into his bed before he retires to his bedroom for the night? If he is a gentleman, he will not shrink from his duty!"

Although deeply shocked by the precision of these counsels, Hedwige de Träxern found them to be excellent and put them into practice.

One night, when all the château was fast asleep, she climbed out of bed, let down her hair, perfumed herself, and on tiptoe, a candle in her hand, entered her husband's apartments. Having reached his bedchamber, she saw a strip of light beneath the door. She set her candlestick down upon a console-table, slipped out of her nightgown and, like Aphrodite rising from the waves, suddenly appeared before the horror-stricken eyes of Léonard, who was quietly reading in his bed. When he saw this shameless creature rushing towards him and felt himself being devoured by her fevered kisses, he emitted a series of strident shrieks which awakened the entire household. The bedchamber was immediately invaded by half a dozen servants, who were convinced their master was being murdered. They stood like statues, stupefied. Mathias, having also run in, appeared to be struck down with consternation. At last he managed to send the flunkeys away and coldly suggested to his sister that she return to her own bedchamber. She had snatched one of the coverlets from the bed and wrapped herself in it. Her dignity restored by this summary tunic, Hedwige began to argue, invoking her wifely privileges and declaring that she would not stir from the spot until she had obtained satisfaction. Her brother finally picked her up in his arms and deposited her bodily in the hallway, then returned to calm Léonard, who, profoundly affected by this scene, spoke of repudiating this Messalina at once. Mathias spent the night at his bedside in order to persuade him that he must at any cost avoid a greater scandal, which would certainly occur if he attempted to annul his marriage. They would have trouble enough keeping the servants quiet as it was! Mathias suggested to his friend that he and his wife take a journey together. Their absence would cause this incident to be forgotten and perhaps, in foreign parts, Hedwige would meet certain agreeable strangers with whom she might satiate in secret the monstrous instincts she had revealed. This solution seemed entirely rational, and two days later a delighted Mathias accompanied the couple to the railroad station. A moment before the train's departure, he whispered into his brother-in-law's ears:"Since you will be in Switzerland, be very careful: accidents can happen so easily in the mountains!"

Count de Träxern stared at his friend in astonishment.

What did this advice mean, and how was he meant to interpret it? Was it a counsel of prudence, or of temerity? Evidently, if a misfortune should occur to Hedwige, his situation would be simplified, and the idea of the murder gradually took root in his mind. Since his wife's extravagant behaviour, he had conceived a veritable horror of her, and lived in the constant apprehension that such a scene might recur. Yet Hedwige seemed pacified: she assumed the disconsolate expression of all forsaken lovers, and daydreamed listlessly. On the pretext of diverting her, Léonard encouraged her to make several excursions with tourists from their hotel, hoping that a chance crevice might engulf the entire "rope" of mountaineers. From a salon window he anxiously watched for their return, counting and recounting the tiny black figures silhouetted on the snowy horizon. He urged her, too, to take the telepheric railway in order to avoid the fatigue of the ascents, but no cables broke that year.

After having exhausted all the dangers of the mountainside, Léonard, only slightly discouraged, decided to try his luck at sea. An enormous yacht was outfitted in order to visit the Mediterranean coast, but neither the sight of the Bay of Naples nor the passage of the Straits of Messina, nor even the entrance into the Golden Horn moved the Countess de Träxern to the point of causing her to lose her head and footing. A trip to Spain produced no better results. At the peril of his own life, Léonard exposed his wife's to diverse vicissitudes, but here, too, neither the bulls of Pamplona nor the brigands of Andalusia seconded his designs. As a last shift, he persuaded Hedwige to board a dirigible which had already suffered several accidents. Alas, this engine was struck down by a storm before reaching Friedrichschafen, where Count Zeppelin himself was to have done the honours of the ascent. The failure of these attempts distressed Léonard all the more in that echoes began to reach him of the successes Mathias Ratkovitz was enjoying in Vienna. In his anxiety, he decided to return to

Siérakov without further delay and to give up any attempt to rid himself of Hedwige for the moment. The fears which his fickle brother-in-law's conduct inspired were well founded, for awaiting him at Siérakov Léonard found a letter from Mathias announcing his engagement to a daughter of a mediatized Prince. This news delighted the heart of the Countess de Träxern and broke her husband's. It was in vain that he pleaded with, then threatened his friend. The latter would agree to no proposal and vowed he would never return to Siérakov, where he had wasted, he claimed, the best years of his youth. To the paean of deliverance Léonard replied by maledictions, borrowed, like his former endearments, from the mystical language he employed in moments of exaltation. The "true life" became a "cursed hyena"; the "beloved" was nothing more than a "vicious reptile to be abandoned to birds of prey". He realized at last that he had been the victim of a machination intended to despoil him of a share of his fortune, and his rage at such exploitation increased his despair at having been betrayed in his sentiments. He swore to obtain revenge and, returning to his earlier intention of a divorce, consulted one of the most famous lawyers in Vienna. The latter made no attempt to conceal the fact that the matter would be a difficult one, for if anyone had cause to sue for divorce it was not the Count but the Countess de Träxern: could she not, after all, invoke her husband's culpable negligence in fulfilling his conjugal duties?

"The only means of solving this problem would be to reverse it," the illustrious jurist informed him. "You must surprise your wife in the very act of adultery."

"But what you say is impossible!" Léonard exclaimed. "She loves me madly!"

"And you complain of that!" his interlocutor replied, restraining a smile. "But are you certain that if Madame de Träxern were to meet another man, an attractive stranger, for instance, she would remain indifferent to the inveiglements of

an adventure? One never knows! Certain of my female
clients, when they wish to rid themselves of a husband either
too zealous or too prudent in his infidelities, ask certain spe-
cialized agencies to obtain for them pretty and extremely qual-
ified chambermaids whose only role is to cause the importun-
ate husband to succumb. The day of his fall, the relatives of
the flouted wife are notified in advance, a bailiff is sent for, and
in the presence of all the servants an affidavit is drawn up in
due form. You see how simple it is! For you, the affair will be
precisely the same, with this one difference, that you must engage a footman rather than a chambermaid. Here is the address of a reliable establishment which will be glad to do you
this little service. . . ."

This notion affected Léonard as a shaft of light in the darkness. He straightway paid the lawyer's honararium without a
glance at the amount, and hastened to the address he had been
given. He was received in a small, discreet salon by a lady still
more discreet. She immediately grasped the situation and
promised to send forthwith to Siérakov an irresistible chauffeur who was as capable of accelerating the workings of hearts
as those of horseless carriages. She stipulated only that the
Count send the man back once he had fulfilled his mission, for
the fine weather was drawing on, and during the summer
Hermann enjoyed a great vogue among lady clients who engaged his company for sentimental journeys. Léonard, enchanted, paid once again, offered his thanks and hurried off to
buy a Mercedes double-phaeton which would justify the presence of a chauffeur at Siérakov.

Fifteen days later, both Hermann and the car disembarked
from the train, one as alluring as the other. The man's superb
carriage was a guarantee of certain success.

"A week will no doubt be enough for him. . . ." the direc-
tress of the agency had assured the Count, when he had asked
her how long the conquest of his wife would take.

As a matter of fact, it required only five days for the seductive chauffeur to make that of his master.

On the sixth, the Countess de Träxern drowned herself in the pond, and on the seventh her husband left Siérakov, driven off in the double-phaeton upon roads more perilous than those of northern Moravia.